A DANGEROUS DECISION

"I won't have my boy carried off to jail for simple foolishness." Justin Harper nodded to his men.

"You can't shoot me down here in the yard," I said. "Leave it be, man, before it just gets worse."

Harper scowled, and it occurred to me—about ten seconds too late—that what I'd told him was that if they started shooting at all, they were gonna have to shoot everybody on the place, and not just me. And it looked like old man Harper was willing to do that to save his boy from hanging.

Harper gave the nod.

Damn him.

Soft and low he said, "Take him, boys. Take him quiet if you can. Take him and we'll use a knife."

FRANK RODERUS
CHARLIE
~ AND ~
THE SIR

LEISURE BOOKS NEW YORK CITY

A LEISURE BOOK®

December 2001

Published by

Dorchester Publishing Co., Inc.
276 Fifth Avenue
New York, NY 10001

ISBN 0-8439-4948-1

The name "Leisure Books" and the stylized "L" with design are trademarks of Dorchester Publishing Co., Inc.

Printed in the United States of America.

Visit us on the web at www.dorchesterpub.com.

For Franklin and Sharon

CHARLIE AND THE SIR

CHAPTER 1

You'd think a fellow would learn to take his own advice. Why, I don't know how many youngsters I've advised, those that were damn fool enough to want to leave the comfort of their mamas and go off to make a hand of themselves, to put their concentration on the workings of the bovine mind and let the human type take care of itself. To just plain butt out, in fact, on anything that don't have to do with the job.

I still think that's pretty good advice. And maybe someday I'll learn to take it myself. Maybe.

The way I hooked up with this Sir, for instance, I just wasn't following my own rules for getting along.

It was down in Cheyenne. You prob'ly know the place. Grass country. Big grass. Enough of it to feed half the steers in the known world, and right there astraddle of the U.P. tracks this ripsnorter of a town where spurs are just naturally part of a man's attire and won't anybody look down on him if he smells a little of horse sweat and wood smoke. I like Cheyenne.

I was there this time because I'd hired on with John Hanks to help him drive a herd of stockers, mostly twos and coming threes, up from the Llano River country. We delivered them to a stubborn old fossil who was rebuilding after the big die-up of the past winter, and I got paid off at Bosler. The trail crew split up there, looking for a blowout or looking for more work or just plain looking.

There wasn't all that much work to be had from horseback, the country right then being short on cows after the die-up and therefore long on unemployed hands. I don't know what happened to the other boys. Me, I drifted down toward Cheyenne. Like I said, I like the place.

So I was there doing some serious loafing until some work opened up, and this particular afternoon I kind of wandered down to the U.P. depot. Watching the puffers come in is a fair entertainment, and there's always the chance that some young lady will get caught beside a vent and have to scramble to keep her skirts from flying high. So I picked me out a soft-looking bench, gave my hat a tilt so as it wouldn't be obvious where I was looking and settled in for a bit.

The early afternoon westbound was something of a disappointment. The only ladies that got off was of the shady variety, and they don't count for ankle watching even if the engineer did blow off a puff of steam at the right moment and got a couple of them to squealing.

Still, I'm nothing if not a stayer, so I sat where I was until the westbound was off-loaded and reloaded and pulled onto a siding so the afternoon eastbound could get to the platform too.

The pickings was kind of slim on that one too, and I believe I rested my eyes a moment or two after the passengers was off.

Next thing I paid attention to, the baggage handlers had some of those little-wheeled carts down at the far, uncovered end of the platform. I noticed that they and a gaggle of those damned brakemen was giving a hoorawing to some skinny, fancy-dressed fellow down there.

Now I know better than to nose into other folks's business. I really do, as I've already tried to explain. But this poor little fellow was looking like he needed some help, and anyway, I've never cared much for railroadmen in general or for brakemen in particular. I don't know if you've noticed this, but they are a rough-talking, rough-acting crowd, and they always seem to herd up together.

One of them will start something and the next one thinks he's got to top that, and you never know where they'll end up. Loud bunch too and braggers, even though, or maybe because, they got so little to brag about.

Anyway, a bunch of them was gathered around this skinny fellow and giving him the hooraw. Making fun of his kit, which looked to be taking up two whole baggage carts all by itself, and poking some fun at him too.

Now I got to admit that the man was dressed odd. From top to bottom he looked different. Up top he had on this silly-looking hard hat that had like a dome with narrow brims on the sides and longer bills front and rear. Then he had on a tweed coat that had been patched at the elbows with scraps of leather, and a wide-collared shirt. No necktie. Instead, he was wearing a silly-looking kerchief of some sort in front of his throat. It looked at first glance like a bandage, but it wasn't.

His britches was just as odd. Light brown and nice enough made, but real funny-shaped. They were wide below the pockets, but from the knees down was fitted close as a spare layer of skin. Heckuva strange way to cut a pair of pants, but it let him get his boots over the bottoms of them easy, so maybe there was something to the idea. And I got to say that the man had a nice pair of boots, tall and black and shiny new, even if the heels was low-like for walking and the toes round. I did admire those boots.

The man himself, like I said, was on the skinny side, although taller than I'd first thought. Almost as tall as me, and I'm something over six feet myself.

He sure was skinny, though. Not much bigger around than the cane he was carrying, which, combined with how thin he was, made me think he'd been sick and come out here to get over the consumption or whatever.

Be that as it may, he must have been outdoors some in the recent past because he was tanned in the face and a bit freckled too. His hair was a kind of blond with now and then a hint of red in it, and he had this little bitty mustache, so pale you couldn't hardly see it and not much thicker than a lead pencil.

His eyes, which I couldn't see until later, you understand, but I'll mention them while I'm on the subject, was pale too. To the point where you had trouble trying to decide if they were blue or gray. I finally settled on blue, but the truth was that they were so pale it didn't hardly make any difference what you wanted to call them.

Anyway, here was this quiet, inoffensive-looking little fellow who was probably an invalid getting a ragging from a bunch of damned railroad brakemen whose manners had got run over on the rails somewhere between Omaha and Salt Lake City.

They was poking fun at the way he was dressed—which I got to admit *was* funny, except you don't say that to an invalid's face—and at the amount of gear he was traveling with and such things as that. Rude is what they were.

Well, I hadn't anything better to do, all the young ladies already being long since off the eastbound and no more trains scheduled through for a while, and anyway, I've never been so fond of brakemen. So I stood and tipped my hat back where it belonged and sidled over to join the crowd.

I stopped there beside them and pretended a yawn and stretched my bones some, which is kind of a polite way of showing them something without bragging about it.

You see, I am not exactly what you would call a little fellow myself. I mean, I don't want to take on too big about it or anything, but the simple fact is that I've never needed help to wrassle down a feisty long-yearling steer, and most fellows that aren't so far riled that they lose their good sense tend to hush up when I tell them that I want them to. If you get what I mean.

So I stretched and yawned and gave those brakemen an eye, and they settled down right smart.

All except for one of them who wasn't quite ready for the fun to end. He looked at his pals—there was half a dozen of them or so, which likely helped make him feel brave—and reached out thinking to snatch the skinny invalid's hat away from him.

The brakeman had to step forward to do that though, and somehow our feet got tangled up so that I was standing on top of his foot. Him being a railroader and not wearing pointy-toed boots, the kind designed so that a hoof can come down on your foot without it doing more than peeve you, I expect it hurt him some, and he let out a squawk.

Before he could say anything that I might've resented and felt obliged to get mad about, I gave him a real surprised, happy look and bellowed, "Why, it's m' old pal Bert."

Now I'd never seen this yahoo before, and the last Bert I'd known was a boy who paid off with me in Bosler and said he was heading down Denver way, but it stopped whatever this fella was going to say next.

I latched an arm around his shoulders and gave him a squeeze, kind of until I could feel his arms scrunch together toward the middle and he began to gasp trying to breathe, and then I looked surprised and turned loose of him.

"Why, you ain't Bert after all."

He puffed a little and took in some air, and when he could talk again, admitted that he wasn't my old pard Bert, so I apologized to him.

"Why don't you boys go on about your work now," I suggested. "I know the U.P. must be payin' you for somethin'. So you boys go on an' do it, and I'll help this little fella get settled."

I smiled at the bunch of them, from one face to the next, and a couple of them gave me weak smiles back, and then they all turned and drifted back toward whatever it is brakemen do when they have their feet on God's good earth.

Once the brakemen were gone, I gave the baggage handlers a looking over and suggested that they get a move on. "This gentleman don't need to be left standing here in the hot sun all the afternoon, you know."

It didn't take the handlers much time at all to finish with the little fellow's stuff.

The little fellow gave me this funny look, funny odd that is and not funny ha-ha, but before he said whatever was on his mind—I know he was going to thank me, but that sort of thing is generally kind of embarrassing—I asked him, "D'you need a buggy to get you over to the hotel? It's three, four hundred yards an' hot walking. I could fetch you a buggy if you like. There's generally some hanging out around the front of the depot."

He looked kind of amused for some reason, but all he said was, "No, thank you." It came out more like 'thenk yew' than 'thank you,' but I could make out what he meant.

I think he was going to say more, but like I explained I'm not real comfortable about folks being grateful, so I turned and got the baggage handlers to moving again.

"You boys trundle that stuff over to the hotel now," I told them, "and be *careful* about it. Pretty leather like that don't need to be scuffed up by the likes of you. You treat that stuff gentle, now."

One of them gave me kind of a dirty look, but him and I both knew that it wouldn't go any farther than that, so I didn't particularly mind.

I turned back to the invalid and shifted over to the side away from his cane and said, "If you won't let me get you a buggy, I reckon the least I can do is walk alongside you. You know. T' make sure you're all right."

There was some sun wrinkles at the corners of his eyes,

and they kind of crinkled and got deeper, I noticed. "Thenk yew," he said again.

"Down this way," I said and pointed.

He must have got rested while he was on the train, because he was able to carry the cane instead of leaning on it. And in fact he set a right brisk pace walking down to the hotel so that I had to stretch a bit myself to keep up with him.

CHAPTER 2

I made sure he was safe to the doors of the hotel and stopped there. "The folks inside'll take care of you now," I assured him. " 'Bye." I turned and headed off.

"Wait," he said.

I turned back to him, and those wrinkles had got deeper again. He smiled and extended a hand, which of course I shook.

"I shouldn't be ungrateful for all your, uh, help, Mister . . . ?" He let it hang there like a question, so I obliged him.

"Charlie Roy," I told him. "Charles Montgomery Roy is the long way around it, but everybody calls me Charlie."

"My pleasure, Mr. Roy." He smiled. "Excuse me. Charlie. I am Arthur Williford Cooke-Williams."

"Nice t' know you, Arthur. I'll bet you're one of them Englishmen. I'd heard there was a bunch of you fellas in this part o' the country."

"I am British, yes."

I grinned at him. "I never met a real live Englishman before now, mostly coming from down south of here where there ain't so many of you. You ain't one of them big-time investors I've heard so much about, are you?"

"Uh, no."

"Well, I didn't think so, but I thought I'd ask." I grinned at him again. "A fella never knows when he'll run into somebody lookin' to hire a hand."

"You are seeking employment, Mr. Roy?"

I shrugged. "I still got near twenty dollars in my kick, so I can still have me some fun before I got to fret about it. An' if nothing else turns up, I can always ride the grub-line south to where there's work. There's places that still have more cattle than they know what t' do with, and a fellow that knows how to build a loop can always catch on down there."

"But you are now, uh, between engagements?"

"Oh, I never been engaged to nobody."

He smiled. "Between jobs then?"

"That I am," I said, although I'd thought I'd already just said that.

"As it happens, Mr. Roy . . . Charlie . . . I have need of someone. My batman left me in San Francisco. Rather too many tales about gold, I should think. May I inquire if you can drive a team?"

"If it can be done with horses, I reckon I can do it, though I'm more comfortable forking 'em than dragging along behind. But if it's work as can be done with horseflesh, I can do 'er."

"Do you happen to know the country?"

"Huh. Anywheres from Sonora to Calgary an' from the Big Muddy to the big mountains. If I ain't been there yet, I ought to."

The invalid rubbed his chin for a moment, then he smiled. "I believe we might be able to work something out, Charlie."

"One thing you got to know, Arthur. I'm a top hand if I do say so myself. I don't work for nothing but forty a month an' keep. I won't budge off that."

"Actually," it came out sounding closer to 'ektually' but again I could make it out, "I had in mind something more like fifty of your dollars per month."

"Since you put it that way, Arthur, I reckon I'm open to negotiation after all."

The little fellow smiled and extended his hand. Which again I shook.

"Done," he said.

Huh. I damn near was done too, though that wasn't his fault.

CHAPTER 3

He'd said he wanted to talk to me over dinner—his treat —and that he wanted to get cleaned up first, though I couldn't see that he looked all that mussed after the train trip, so I left him at the hotel with all the junk he was hauling and went back to the room I'd taken at Mrs. Feaster's boarding house.

The boarding house was about what you'd expect in a cow town. Clean and cheap and it came with meals included. I generally make it a point to find a place like that when I'm between jobs and pay something in advance so I won't get thrown out hungry when my money runs out or I'm taken bad with drink or something. Mrs. Feaster was a poor cook, but her hired girl Angela was a plump, pretty thing with always a smile and a laugh, so all in all it was a pretty fair kind of place. I was paid for another three days there, so I didn't have to put the sneak on to get up to my room or nothing.

My roommate—it cost a dollar a week extra for a room all to yourself, an' after sharing blankets on cow drives for near about all the years I could remember, privacy wasn't all that important to me—was out for the evening already, so I slicked my hair back with some water and put the borrow on the fella's bay rum so as to make myself presentable for dinner with the invalid.

I would've changed to a fresh shirt too, except that my laundry—which is another thing I like to do when I'm going to be in one spot for a while and still have money in my kick—wasn't back yet. So I settled for brushing off as

best I could and stopped downstairs to black my boots
with some soot from the stove and some grease that Angela slipped me without Mrs. Feaster knowing.

When I was done preening, I tucked my shirttail in
good and stood up straight for Angela to look me over.
"What d'you think?"

"You need a shave, Charlie."

"Aw, I just shaved this morning." Although when I felt
my face I had to admit there was some scratchy stubble
there. "Twice in one day, I'd get all raw an' dried out."

"All right." She leant a little closer and said, "You do
smell awful pretty though."

I gave her a wink and a grin, thinking maybe her and
me could discuss that later on in the evening, like after she
got done working.

"You got a date tonight, Charlie?" There was something
in her voice that told me what she was hoping the answer
would be.

"Naw, I'm just supposed to see some Englishman about
a new job. That's all."

"One of those English gentlemen?" This time her voice
was saying that maybe I wasn't the *only* one she could be
interested in this evening.

I shrugged. "I guess so."

"Is he a lord, Charlie? One of those titled gentlemen?"

"Heck, I dunno. I never asked."

"You should, Charlie. My girlfriend Tibby works at the
Club, and she met a gentleman there who's a marquis,
Charlie. Can you imagine that? A real marquis. And he's
ever so rich and he told her that he wants to take her back
to England with him and . . ."

"Come on now, Angela. You know better'n that. Your
girlfriend ought to too."

She gave me a pout.

Personally I wasn't so fond of the way this conversation
was going anyhow, so I gave my hair another swipe with

my palm and set my hat comfortable and headed for the door.

"You're mad at me, aren't you?" Angela asked of my back.

"Naw, I ain't mad at you." But I guess I was, a little. Marquis, indeed. The only marquis I'd ever heard of was the Queensberry one, and I couldn't feature him showing up in Cheyenne with a yen to carry some cleaning girl or whatever off to England with him.

Arthur'd told me to meet him at the hotel about eight and it was still early, so I dawdled along and admired all the stuff in the store windows and stopped in at the Bullhead for a small snort.

There was a couple of early evening drunks having an argument about whether manilla or rawhide makes the best catch rope. I stepped around them and put down my fifteen cents for a whiskey.

The barman delivered it and gave a scowl to the drunks, who were getting loud.

"You fellows quiet down now. This is a respectable place."

One of the drunks said something that I couldn't possibly set down where a lady might see, and the both of them decided to get mad at the barman.

They made a lunge for the fella, and he grabbed for a bungstarter and about then all the other fellas at the bar began looking for a quieter spot where they could do their drinking.

The barman came up with his bungstarter and both the drunks took hold of him, and one of them wrassled the club away from him and it was beginning to look like it could get nasty.

"Excuse me a minute boys." I took hold of the nearer of the two, the one that had the bungstarter now, and kind of picked him up and plucked the stick out of his hand. "You don't wanta cause any trouble now."

The fella gave me this pale, big-eyed look and went to trying to punch and kick, which would have mussed me up before my dinner with Arthur, so I turned him around and kind of tossed him on top of his buddy and the both of them went down in a tangle of arms and legs.

They came up still proddy, which shows what too much liquor will do for a person, but by now the barman had his bungstarter back and was fixing to bust their heads for them. That didn't seem hardly right as they was only drunk and not truly mean, so I pulled him off them and set him back behind his bar where he belonged.

"Now dang it, you fellas all settle down here before somebody gets hurt."

There was some grunting and grumbling, but the barman was certainly willing to have things quiet and the drunks didn't seem so inclined to stay at it once they gave me a good looking over. Neither one of them came up to my chin, hardly.

"What if we don't wanta?" one of them muttered.

"Why if that was so, I expect I'd have to get peeved and maybe mess up my only clean shirt. You don't want to make me do that."

The one acted like maybe he did, but his buddy was sobering up now and took him by the arm and pulled him out of there for greener pastures. Or at least for safer ones.

"Thanks," the barman said.

"De nada." I tasted the whiskey finally. It wasn't bad.

"You want a refill? It's on the house."

"No, but I might take you up on that later."

"I'll be here. The offer's good anytime."

"Thank you." The clock on the wall, which was protected against flying objects by a wire-mesh cage, showed that it was near eight, so I finished my drink and wandered over to the hotel.

CHAPTER 4

The restaurant at the hotel was some kind of fancy.

I'd not been there before, of course, and it sure wasn't anything like what I expected, whatever that was.

I mean, the fellows waiting on the tables was all wearing stiff collars and black coats with shiny lapels, and just the stuff set out on the tables looked like it belonged in a jewelry store. There wasn't any tin or crockery ware at all here but real silver and china and linen and chandeliers and . . . fancy, that's all. Extra fancy.

It looked like the kind of place that would cost a week's wages to eat one meal at.

The gentlemen sitting at the tables was all dressed to the nines, looking even fancier than the waiters did, and at a couple of the tables there was ladies too. The real thing, you could tell, in gowns and hats, dressed up like they was fixing to go to a ball afterward.

Shee-oot!

I could see Arthur sitting at a small table over by the windows. I waved and headed toward him, and about that time a stiff-necked fella in a coat with swallow tails and a tie so snug it would choke a goat snagged me by the elbow.

"See here now, my good man, just where do you think you are going?"

"Right over there." I pointed to where Arthur was, sitting there dressed just as dandy as any of the rest of them while a black-coated waiter poured wine into his glass.

"I should say not," stiff-neck said. "We do not serve," his lips twisted into a bit of a sneer, *"gentlemen* without coat and tie here."

Now I might not be fancy, and I do try and not get mad without good reason, but I'm not so stupid that I don't know when I'm being looked down on.

"I think you're gonna make an exception this one time," I told him just as polite as I knew how but with something of an edge in my voice.

"No exceptions," stiff-neck said. "I shall have to ask you to leave."

I smiled at him and reached down to straighten his tie and pull it even tighter than it already was.

He got the message, I guess. He held himself extra stiff, and his eyes started cutting back and forth as if to see who all was handy to back him—though I happened to notice that all the fancy waiters was suddenly real attentive to their customers and didn't seem to notice stiff-neck's problem—but I got to give the guy credit. He swelled his chest out just as far as he was able, and he looked like he wasn't willing to back down any.

Whatever it was that stiff-neck figured to do, he didn't have to.

I'd no sooner got done adjusting stiff-neck's tie than Arthur was there taking stiff-neck's hand off my elbow and talking smooth as butter.

"The gentleman will be dining at my table, John." He leaned over and whispered something into stiff-neck John's ear, and the guy's eyes bugged a little, and when he turned back to me, danged if he didn't give me a funny little half bow, sort of, and personally escorted me over to Arthur's table.

Held the chair out for me to sit and everything, even snapped a napkin open and draped it on my lap and snapped his fingers to bring a waiter on the double quick to pour a glass of wine that I didn't particularly want.

Stiff-neck bowed to me again and then to Arthur, and he said, "At your pleasure, Sir Arthur."

Arthur was sitting kind of stiff himself now, with his nose kinda stuck up in the air. He gave stiff-neck the barest hint of a nod and waved the fella away, and old stiff-neck scuttled off toward the front in a hurry.

I have to admit that I was impressed, particularly since to my certain knowledge Arthur hadn't been in town more'n a few hours and was already calling stiff-neck by his first name and ordering him about.

"What'd you tell that fella when you whispered in his ear?" I asked.

A hint of a smile showed just for a second and then was gone. "Why, I explained to him who you are, Charlie."

"Huh?"

There wasn't any smile this time. Just as solemn and serious as a body could want, Arthur said, "I told him you are a millionaire cattle baron, of course. An *eccentric* millionaire cattle baron, actually."

It's a good thing I didn't have a mouthful of wine or anything at the time. I'd've sprayed it all over the table and Arthur too when I busted out laughing.

"You told him that? Really?"

Arthur shrugged.

"Shee-oot," I said and grinned.

It occurred to me something that old stiff-neck had said and that that darned Angela had said too. "He called you Sir Arthur. Are you really one of them Sirs? Like with a title an' all that?"

"Uh, ektually . . . yes. The knighthood only, however. I have no title. Uh, second son and all that."

Whatever *that* meant. I guess I was supposed to understand it, but I didn't.

"You're a real Sir, though, huh?"

"Uh . . . yes."

"I'll be damned."

This time he did smile. "Hopefully not."

"Well, who'd'a guessed it. Me working for a real Sir." I chuckled and tasted some of the wine, which looked like soda pop but didn't taste all that bad.

Arthur—Sir Arthur I guess I shoulda been calling him, though I'd already got the habit of just thinking of him as plain Arthur—crooked a finger and almost like magic there was a waiter at the table bowing and scraping and practically aquiver to see what he could do for the English Sir an' the millionaire cattle baron.

Him and Arthur went into a conference on what Arthur would have for supper, though for all I could tell of it they might've been talking a different language. When it came my turn to order, I asked for my usual fancy-time, night-out meal, which is a tallow-fried steak cooked near to burning but with the taters mashed and gravy-covered instead of the ordinary trail style which is boiled and otherwise dry. The waiter acted like that was just about the finest, most sensible order he'd ever heard delivered. But then he'd acted that way about Arthur's order too.

"Shall we discuss our impending venture?" Arthur asked once the waiter was out of the way.

I took it that he meant we was to talk about what I was to do in exchange for drawing pay from him, so I nodded. "It's your party, Arthur."

Of course as it turned out, it wasn't no kind of party at all, but I wouldn't've avoided it if I could have.

CHAPTER 5

The Sir—I don't know why it tickled me so, this skinny little invalid being a Sir, but it did—sure wasn't a man for moving light and fast. Lordy, I reckon not.

First thing I had to do was go out an' find a rig and team big enough for hauling all his bags and trunks and boxes and crates that'd come in on the train with him, the same huge pile o' stuff that those railroaders had been so amused by. Which you would think would be easy enough most anyplace but wasn't, not with what all Arthur wanted of his traveling rig.

First off, he said, it had to haul everything. Easy enough, of course. Any old freight wagon would handle that. But there was more that he wanted outa his transportation.

The rig also had to have accommodations. That's what he called it. Accommodations. So he could live outa the thing without having to fuss with setting up a tent and cot and carpet and such, each an' every night.

Did you ever hear of such a thing? Tents and cots and carpets? Shee-oot! Most of my life I've spent following around behind the back end of some cow, and except for when I've wintered over at a line camp or working out of a bunkhouse, I've never wanted more'n a flat place to lay out by bedroll. Those times, that is, that I owned a bedroll. Some of the time it's just been a saddle blanket laid out on the ground and it was bed enough just like a roof of stars is ceiling enough.

Anyhow, the invalid wanted a wagon that he could live out of, with his cot and comforts kept ready. I didn't say anything about that, as I figured he prob'ly had his reasons, what with being an invalid and all. Maybe it was something his doctors'd told him he had to do.

Then on top of all *that* he wanted an outfit tough enough to take off where there wasn't any roads, as he said he wanted to do some "collecting" on the way to wherever it was we was going.

Collecting.

That's what he said.

Now what a man could expect to "collect" on the grassy plains, except maybe saddle sores and sunburn, I just couldn't figure.

Still, it was his deal, and at fifty dollars hard money a month, he was entitled to be just about as dotty as he pleased, so I told him I'd see what I could do.

I looked first at all the obvious places. The livery and the wagon yards and the freight-hauling companies and such as that. Turned out there was plenty of rigs available for sale in Cheyenne. Big freight wagons, little wagons, buckboards, buggies, carriages, even a fancy-wheeled brougham that some idjit had had hauled in from someplace.

One of the yards even had a couple covered-top Conestogas and Studebakers to sell. One of them might've been just the ticket, except that by the time an outfit got as far as Cheyenne—and then got *left* there—it wasn't likely to be of much use for anything except firewood, and these was no exception to that rule.

They were all rickety, ancient old things with the frames dried out and ready to bust and axles that were rough, raw, makeshift affairs. On one of them the poor sap who'd nursed it this far out from Missoura had actually gone and *nailed* the tires in place. They were pitiful, though I guess not so much so as the rig sitting next to that one in the sale yard. That outfit used to be a pretty nice old boat shaped Conestoga at one time, but things must've gone bad for the owner of it for all that was left was the front half of the thing. The back part had been sawed clean off and left someplace so that all that was left was like a giant cart, sorta like those big old freight carretas that they use down in New Mexico and Sonora.

Anyway, there wasn't a dang thing I could find in Cheyenne that looked like it would do what Arthur wanted. I went back and told him so that next afternoon.

He took it easy enough, smoothing his mustache with a fingertip and smiling like he hadn't a care in the world.

"Do you have any suggestions, Charles?"

"Well now, I have to say that I've been giving it some thought, Arthur, and I recall seein' some rigs over by Bosler that might fit the bill. Sheepherder's wagons, somebody said they was. They come all fitted out with beds an' stoves an' they're plenty tough, I expect. One of them might do."

"Then by all means, Charles, go purchase one."

"Bosler is . . ."

"I know where it is, Charles. The train from San Francisco passed through there."

"You don't wanta . . ."

"Here." He up and pulls out a wallet that's just choked with folding money, some of it bigger than what I was used to and kinda funny-looking, and peels off more of a wad than I've ever seen in my entire lifetime. Peels it off and just hands it over to me.

I counted it, and there was five hundred dollars there. Five. Hundred. Dollars.

I got shaky just staring at it there in the palm of my hand.

I'd never held so much money in my hand all at one time, of course. It was more'n a year's pay for an ordinary waddie. And I've never known any waddie, me included, who was able to save more than two or three dollars from one payday to the next.

This Sir, though, he never seemed to hardly give it a thought. He handed it right over to me and all he said was, "Do you think that will be enough to cover the purchase?"

I gulped and felt like my collar was too tight, even though I wasn't wearing one and had the top button of my shirt loose. "Sure," I told him.

Arthur smiled like everything was all settled.

"Dang it, Arthur, you shouldn't ought to flash a roll like that. Somebody could bop you over the head an' rob you blind. Why, you shouldn't even of give it to me. I mean, I sure ain't gonna do anything to do you hurt, but you can't know that for sure. You don't hardly know me from Adam's off ox, Arthur."

He didn't smile again exactly, but the wrinkles at the corners of his eyes got deeper. "Go to Bosler, Charles, and get our wagon. If you need more money, let me know."

I know it sounds silly to say so, when the man was being so trusting of me, but I was actually feeling just a bit exasperated with this strange Sir. Began to think, in fact, that he was maybe a bit weak in the head as well as weak in the body and that he was going to need a power of looking after.

Still, I'd hired on with the man. I would do what was needed, including protecting the poor fella if it came to that. Which I was beginning to think it just might.

"There's a night train," was all I told him though. "I'll be on it an' get back here quick as I can."

"Do that, Charles. And thenk yew."

Once again the crinkles at the corners of his eyes got deeper, but he didn't say anything.

I stuffed all that money down deep in my pocket—it'd be safe enough with me, I figured, for who would ever guess that an ordinary poke would be carrying such a roll

—and headed for the train station to see when the next local westbound was due out. Carrying so much money, though, made me begin to wish that I owned a gun to guard it with.

CHAPTER 6

Since I had leftover money in my pockets from my last job and a new one already in hand, I was tempted to have myself a blowout in Bosler that night. But I had the Sir's money too, and the truth is that I guess I just didn't trust myself to take care of it while getting rid of my own. So I ignored the temptations and settled for getting a good night's sleep out by the loading pens alongside the rails. Kinda depressing, really.

The pens was empty when I bedded down that night, but along about dawn I got woke up by the sound of bleating and snorting coming at me out o' the half-light. Startling is what it was.

I came upright in the bedroll I'd brought along from Cheyenne and blinked, and there come more dang sheep than you would think could live in the whole dang world. Hundreds of the critters, all of them ugly and noisy and stinking and stupid. And all of them looking naked from having been sheared. The owners of them, I guessed, had already taken the wool off them and were selling them now for meat. Or something. I don't pretend to know all that much about sheep.

That is one thing, though. A fella thinks of Wyoming Territory and he just naturally thinks about cows. With grass plains laying way out past the horizons in most any direction you care to look and with all that good water running down off the mountain ranges, you just naturally think of Wyoming as God-given cow country. And of course it is.

But it's also true that the territory has more dang sheep in it than enough.

Somebody told me once that there's more sheep in that country than cows. I don't know whether to believe that or not, but it's what I was told.

After looking at this herd of the critters coming toward me outa the first slant of yella morning light, I know that I can almost believe it if not quite.

I stood up and rolled my bed quick lest those smelly things crowd all over it and went over to open the pen gates for the herders. Unlike some I do try and be polite to those folks and not look down my nose at them.

"Morning."

"Good morning yourself." The man ahorseback stopped by the gate I'd just opened and hollered something in a language I didn't understand—though he didn't look like a foreigner himself—and the sheepherders—who mostly did look foreign—commenced to whistle and wave and make funny motions.

There was a pack of dogs running alongside the herd of sheep, and I have to admit that it was cunning the way those dogs got to work thinning that great glob of sheep into a line and passing them through the gate into the pens.

If a fella could teach dogs to handle cattle like that, why, cowboying would be a sight easier.

Can't be done, of course. They work cows with dogs down in the brush country of south Texas, as I've seen many a time, but about all the dogs are good for is finding those snorty ladinos and chasing them outa the thickets where they like to hide. You can't actually herd with the critters, which is a shame.

These foreign-looking sheep fellas had it figured, though, and it was interesting to watch the dogs do their work for them.

I leaned on the top rail of the pen and took it all in.

The ramrod, who looked about as ordinary as anybody else, sat his horse nearby until he saw that everything was in hand. Then he dismounted and came over to stand beside me.

"Looking for work, mister?"

"No offense, but not that kind even if I was. Which I ain't."

He nodded, not seeming to mind that I was set in my ways when it come to cows over sheep.

"Tell you what, though," I said. "I'm here looking for one of them wagons like you fellas use. You know. With the boxed top and stove and bunks and such. You wouldn't have one to spare, would you?"

"That's a strange thing to ask."

"Maybe, but buying one o' them things is why I came here."

He pulled at his chin some—which needed shaving but no worse than mine did—and appeared to be thinking it over. "I might be able to spare one. If the price is right. Lost some men recently. Two of 'em quit me and another died. Which is why I was asking did you want work. Right now I've got more equipment than people. What did you say you were offering?"

"I got to be honest with you, mister. I don't know what one o' them rigs is worth."

The fella began to smile. Then he took a closer look at me. And I got to say that I did not look my very best, having just crawled out of my bed. My clothes weren't any too swell and were rumpled from sleeping in them anyhow, and my boots were run down at the heel some. Like I said, I needed a shave, and so far hadn't so much as taken a swipe of a hand over my hair. All in all I'd guess that I prob'ly looked pretty seedy. Which of course is just what a body wants when he's fixing to dicker on the purchase of something. I sure didn't look like I'd be carrying any five hundred dollars on me.

"I don't know," the man mused, pulling at his chin again. "A good sheep wagon comes dear."

"Well, I need one. If I can afford it, that is."

He thought on it some more and stared off into space and dug the toe of his boot into the ground and finally said, "I guess I have one that I might let go."

"How much?"

"Hundred and a half. I wouldn't take a penny less."

It was my turn to play the horse trader's game. I looked at the sky for a bit. Then I stuffed my hands into my back pockets and wallowed my boots through the dirt while I peered down at them. I cleared my throat a couple times and spit. Finally I fixed the fella with a look in the eyes.

"That'd be all set up?" I asked.

That made it his turn again. His face twisted till he looked like he was hurting from pondering so hard. He grabbed hold of a pen rail and tugged on it. He paced a few yards off and back again.

I, of course, pretended not to be interested much in all this. I took out my pocket knife and used it to slice a sliver from one of the posts and trimmed the thing to a blunt point so I could clean under my fingernails with it. Like I wasn't paying attention to all this fella was going through.

"Complete," he said finally.

"Horse team," I said. "I don't like having nothing to do with mules."

This time there wasn't any hesitating or playacting. He nodded right off. "Horses," he agreed. "I don't run mules neither."

"If the rig's in decent shape," I said.

"All my equipment is in decent shape, cowboy."

I grinned and held my hand out for him to shake on the deal.

"Done," he said.

And he smiled so big that I guess I'd gone and saved the

Sir 350 bucks, but could've saved him 25 or 50 more if I'd known enough to do it.

Still and all . . .

The fella turned and said something to one of the dark-haired herders who'd come drifting near—one of those Bascos, I guessed without really knowing—and the sheepherder flopped away on his pony, riding like a man who was happier walking than riding.

"I'll be go to hell," I said.

"What's that?"

"Did you see that fella? And some of them others too, now that I notice it. He's only got one spur on."

The bossman grinned. "Saves money that way," he said. "Instead of each man having to buy a set of spurs, they go together and two of them buy one pair. That way they each have spurs for half the price."

"Yeah, but . . ."

He laughed. "I know. It looks funny. But I'll let you in on a secret, cowboy. You get one side of the horse to moving an' the other side comes along at the same speed." He reached into his pocket and offered me a chew before he carved one off for himself. "Try it sometime. I promise you it works."

I shook my head in wonder at the way these sheepmen are.

I got to say, though, that the funny-looking wagon, when they brought it up for me to see, was every bit as good as a body could want. Tight and clean and no bugs in the bedding that I could find. It was drawn by a mismatched pair of heavy cobs that weren't pretty to look at but were built right and looked like they could do the job.

When I opened the door to see inside, a brown and white dog with shaggy hair and blue eyes—I know it sounds strange, but I swear it's so, blue eyes—jumped up inside the little house-on-wheels and wagged its tail.

"What the hell is this?"

The seller grinned and gave me a shrug. "You said set up. That dog's part of the setup. This wagon's the only home it's ever known, and he'll go everyplace it does. Unless you shoot him, of course. I expect you could get rid of him that way."

"Well, I ain't gonna shoot him. Not gonna herd any sheep with him neither, though."

"Whatever you want, friend. He's your dog now."

I wasn't real sure how to take that, actually. I mean, I'd been around dogs some before, of course, but I'd sure never had one of my own to take care of nor anything like it.

I was about to say something about one of the Bascos taking him to work with, tying him up till I got away with the wagon, but the damned critter didn't seem to know that I didn't want him. He kept wagging his tail, right from about the middle of his back onward, and come over to lick at my hand with a sloppy-wet tongue. Now how d'you kick an animal out when it goes and does something like that, I ask you.

Horses are what I'm used to of course, but horses aren't anyways friendly. Mostly stupid, meaner'n hell sometimes, always useful. They're good tools. But friendly? Huh-uh.

As for dogs . . .

I guess what I'm saying is that it was kinda, well, nice the way this brown and white, funny-looking furry thing was making all over me.

So I didn't actually say anything about one of the Bascos keeping him. Instead I told the guy, "I guess I owe you some money, don't I?" And the Sir had his rolling house.

CHAPTER 7

It's a ways from Bosler back down to Cheyenne, call it fifty miles or thereabouts. I suppose I could've made it in one push but that would've been asking a lot of a team I didn't know, so I figured to lay over for a night and make a two-day drive out of it.

I got to say one thing about that fella I bought the Sir's rig from—an' come to think of it I guess I never did actually get his name, not that I figured it mattered—when he sold an outfit that was set up, it was dang sure set up. There was everything a body could need in there, including food enough for a month if a body's tastes ran to simple stuff like rice and cornmeal and embalmed beef.

Anyway . . . I kinda got off track as to what I was saying . . . it was a two-day drive back down to where the Sir was waiting. Gave me a good chance to get familiar with the rig, I figured, and to see if there was any repairs or changes I'd want to make before we left out from Cheyenne to do the Sir's "collecting" and whatever.

Actually, I was looking forward too to having some time alone to just myself and being able to go along as I pleased for a change instead of having to be doing according to what somebody else wanted.

Except that I wasn't near as alone as I'd thought on this trip.

Not that I had company. Exactly. Except that I kinda had company. Does that make sense? I didn't think so.

The thing is, there was this wood flap built over the front bunk. It opened onto the driving box, like for ventilation or passing things through or whatever. And as it was open when I picked the rig up, I just left it that way when I drove off.

Well the next thing I know here comes this speckledy brown and white nose outa the thing with a wet tongue attached to it, and the back of my neck an' then my ears is getting a bath. Which is not to say that I didn't need washing there, but I got to say that at first it startled me. Then when I realized what was what, it tickled. An' I guess I chortled and laughed some and scratched the fool creature behind the ears. I'd never done a thing like that in my life before, and I was kinda glad there wasn't anyone around to see.

Worse, inside three, four miles I went and stopped the rig and went around to open the back door of the thing and let the dog out so he—or she, I hadn't gone and looked—could get up on the seat beside me.

The dang creature sat up on the seat beside me with his ears perky and his tongue hanging out and acted like he owned the outfit. Just as happy as a dead pig in the sunshine.

I scratched him some, and he licked me some and that night after he gave the countryside a good looking over—puzzled, I think, because there wasn't any sheep handy for him to keep track of—he come inside the thing with me an' curled up on the floor right smack beside my bed. I woke up sometime during the night an' found that he'd made better sleeping arrangements for himself while I wasn't looking. He'd gone and snuck up onto the bunk right beside me and was sleeping with his back curled tight against my belly.

Crazy thing.

I know I prob'ly should've kicked him the hell out right there on the spot. But I didn't. I just yawned and scratched him behind the ear and felt his tail thump against the blankets, and both of us went back to sleep.

Next afternoon when I rolled up in front of the hotel to show Arthur what he'd bought, the dog was setting there beside me like we were the oldest and best of friends. If Arthur thought anything odd about me showing up with a mutt he never said anything about it. And neither did I.

CHAPTER 8

"In here, I think. No. No, in here. There is room enough in here. Put it in here."

I sighed and moved everything to where Arthur wanted it. For the third, maybe the fourth time. He sure was a fussbudget when it came to getting all his stuff put where he wanted it.

I got to say, though, that he was agreeable about the rig I'd brought back and about the return of the $350 that I hadn't spent.

"Quite nice" was all he actually said out loud, but I could see in his eyes that he was happy with it. I was beginning to learn that this funny little invalid Sir didn't always say quite everything that he meant and that I had to look close to figure it all out.

"I shall save these rear two cabinets for your personal possessions, Charles. Would that be sufficient?"

I looked at where he was pointing and laughed. "Damn, Arthur, you give me that one little shelf there an' I'm all moved in. Except for my saddle, o' course, and I'll throw that into the possum belly."

"Possum belly?" he repeated. For some reason he looked amused.

"Sure. That canvas sling underneath the wagon. It's really for haulin' wood when you're in bare country, but it's handy for toting bulky stuff like saddles too."

"Possum belly," he said again, mouthing the words slowly like he was committing them to memory.

"Yup. Possum belly." I levered the trunk he was unloading a little further up the narrow aisle that was in the middle of the wagon house so's he could get to it easier. He had said he would stow everything inside the rolling house an' leave his empty trunks and stuff in storage here at the hotel.

I got to say I found it some strange that one man could need so much room for his kit or that the Sir'd thought I should need two whole cabinets all to myself.

Shee-oot, a traveling fella like me generally doesn't own more than he can carry rolled up in his bed and maybe in a pair of saddlebags. That and a saddle, of course. A man can't earn a living without his saddle.

I'd already collected my clean laundry an' told Mrs. Feaster I wouldn't be staying longer. So far as I was concerned we were ready to go anytime Arthur wanted.

"Do you have a horse you wish to bring along, Charles?"

Which kinda showed what he knew, or didn't know, about such things.

Oh, I've known fellas that would insist on owning a horse. But generally that's more nuisance than it's worth. Just something to pay for feeding between jobs. On the job, of course, you use whatever saddle string you're given, and that's that. No need for a horse between jobs and for sure no need for the trouble and expense of one. I didn't try and explain all that to him, though. Just told him that I didn't and let it go at that.

The dog, now that was a different story. I didn't hardly know what to think about the dog. It really went with the rig, not with Arthur nor with me exactly, but I was kinda starting to think of it like it was mine somehow. Silly, but it's so.

"You thinking about moving out right away?" I asked.

"Not necessarily. Is there something you need to do?"

"Well, I notice that there's a hammer in that bottom drawer an' a few shoe nails, but there's no shoes in there. I think I got a spare shoe in my saddlebags, but that's for a cow pony. Wouldn't begin to fit a dinner plate hoof like is on these cobs. I was thinking maybe I should buy a couple to keep on hand just in case we need them."

"By all means," Arthur said. "Purchase whatever you believe we need." He whipped out a fifty-dollar bill, which was ten times what I could possibly need, and didn't say anything about receipts or accounting for it. This old boy had a lot to learn. Not that I figured to take advantage of him, but still . . .

For an invalid he sure was spry, though. While he was unpacking his things and putting them where he wanted, he'd laid his cane aside and was moving around about as good as anybody. I sure couldn't figure the skinny little fella.

At fifty a month, of course, I didn't have to.

I left him to his unpacking and went off to find some big horseshoes and longer nails and maybe a roll of waxed harness thread just in case I had to make some repairs.

The dog trailed along beside me, hanging right there where I could reach down an' rub his head—by now I'd looked, and it was for sure a he—without even having to look to see was he still there.

For some reason that pleased me, and I stopped at a butcher's and got the dumb thing a bone to gnaw on once we got back to the wagon.

CHAPTER 9

I slept in the wagon house that night rather than paying for a room someplace or imposing on Mrs. Feaster after I'd told her I was leaving, so it was no problem to be fed and hitched and outside the hotel by dawn, which was when the Sir said he wanted to leave.

I hadn't any idea that he would actually be ready to *leave* then, of course. You take most dudes, they get all fired up with an idea and want to do it right now and they're gonna be ready to go after it, whatever it is, at the crack of dawn. Sure they are. Most of them, the truth is, find that dawn's a dandy idea of an evening, but not so good come dawn. Most of them, if they wake up at all so early, just want to grunt an' snort and roll over for some more sleep come the actual hour, as I've seen more'n once when an outfit I was with has been "helped" by visitors or distant relatives or whatever. I mean, most of them just plain find it easier to say than to do when it comes to rolling out with the sun.

Damn me, though, if the Sir wasn't setting there on the front porch of the hotel when I got there. Setting there in a rocking chair with his cane in his lap and his overnight valise on the floor beside him, all the rest of his stuff already being packed inside the wagon.

"Good morning, Charles." He sure sounded chipper enough for a dude in the early light, and before I could set the hitch weights and go to help him, he was out of his chair and down to the wagon seeming to move as easy as you please. Maybe this dry, north plains air was good for whatever ailed him.

"Mornin', Arthur." I took his valise and shoved it through the passthrough into the house and gave him a hand up. The dog moved over to make room for him an' sat between us, and that was pretty much to become the way we traveled. Me driving and the Sir riding and the brown and white dog setting nose high and comfortable on the seat between the two of us.

Arthur smiled and rubbed his hands together and looked eager to be off.

He was dressed funny again, I noticed. Wearing that odd-shaped hard hat again and the tight britches, but this time instead of a coat he was wearing a khaki-colored thing that was about half jacket and half shirt and had pockets all over it. I'd never seen anything like it.

"Shall we be off?" he said cheerfully.

"Shore," I told him. "But could I ask you a kinda personal question?"

He frowned and just for a split second hesitated. "If you wish."

I grinned at him. "Where we goin'?"

The invalid blinked and got this blank-faced look about him for a moment. Then he threw his head back an' laughed. "North, Charles. We travel north."

Well, it sure made no nevermind to me. I spanked the team into motion and aimed them for where the north star had disappeared just a little while before.

CHAPTER 10

"Charles!"

"Y' know, Arthur, if it's all the same to you, I druther be called . . ."

"Dammit, man, not now. Stop the vehicle. Quickly."

He did sound kinda excited, I realized now. I had no idea what it was that was getting him so het up, but I pulled the cobs to a halt.

Before we even got stopped Arthur was standing up in the box, grabbing the top of the house to keep from losing his balance and falling out. He was staring off toward the right, past the little roll in the ground we were climbing over.

"There. Do you see? Oh, *jolly* good."

He really seemed excited, but damned if I could tell why that should be.

"Don't you *see* them?"

"All I can see over there, Arthur, is a bunch of dang antelope."

He gave me a sharp look and snapped, "Your North American pronghorn, Charles, is properly categorized as *Antilocapra americana.* And it is *not* an antelope."

Invalid or not, I gave the Sir a dirty look. Here he was, a foreigner, and telling me that an antelope isn't an antelope. And I been seeing those things thick as mosquitoes along a river bank, almost, for about as long as I can remember.

Still, I didn't want to say anything to embarrass him. It wasn't his fault if he didn't know any better.

All I said was, "That's fine, Arthur, but whatever are we stopping for?"

"Why, to collect a specimen, of course. They've seen us, Charles. Back the team down from the crest. Quickly now."

A hunting trip? He'd bought this outfit and was paying me fifty dollars a month, and all he wanted was to go on a hunting trip? Shee-oot.

I leant forward, though, and rewrapped the driving lines on my fists and eased the team backward so that the wagon rolled back downhill to where those antelope—or whatever the hell the Sir wanted to call them—couldn't see what Arthur was up to.

"Capital," Arthur said. He jumped down outa the box, even leaving his cane behind, and ran around to the back of the rig so he could get inside.

I've never been one to trust a horse, any horse, to stay put where I want it to, unless I've got the thing nailed in place, so I dragged out the hitch weights and clipped their leads to the cobs's bits before I followed, the dog staying right at my knee with its tail going like it was looking forward to something too.

Time I got around to the door of the house, Arthur had already dragged out one of the long, flat, leather cases he'd crammed under his bunk and had the thing laid out on top of his covers.

The case turned out to be a gun case with a pair of rifles inside it. And I must say that those were about the prettiest rifles I ever did see. I got no idea what something like that would cost, but if I had to guess, I would say that just one of those rifles would set a man up with a good start on a small herd of stock cows.

One was just as pretty as the other, and they had engraving and silver and gold inlays on their receivers and carvings on the wood and sights—sights that big and complicated needed an engineer to figure them out. I've seen

surveyors' instruments, and those weren't half so complicated as the sights on those two rifles.

Arthur picked one of the things out of the case and kind
of smoothed his hand down along the stock of it and
hefted it up and down a couple times, then laid it aside
and closed the case and returned it to the place under the
bunk where there was a couple other long, flat cases that I
assumed now were more guns.

He dug through a cabinet and brought out a small,
wood case and opened it up, and this one had ammunition
in it. Long, sleek-looking cartridges—I don't know
enough about guns to be able to look at a cartridge and
figure out what size it is, but I know these weren't anything like the squatty little .45s and .44-40s that I'd seen
before—and each one of the things set into holes drilled
into the body of the insides of the case. That too was
something that was new to me.

"Hold these," Arthur said. He handed me a pair of field
glasses and a canvas kit bag that was fairly heavy.

He stuffed some cartridges into one of the pockets on
that jacket-shirt thing he was wearing and took up the
rifle again. "Come along. Quickly now," and he was out
the door and moving at a slow, easy run, running kinda
bent over, just below the crest of the rise we'd been about
to top.

I stopped long enough to see that the horses was all
right and not worrying at their bits, and he called out,
"Quickly," again in a loud, hoarse whisper.

He kept going like that for the better part of a quarter
mile without stopping or even slowing down, and I began
to think that this dry plains air was *really* doing him good.
So dang good that if he didn't stop soon, I was gonna get
winded first and wouldn't *that* be embarrassing.

Eventually, though, he quit and dropped down to his
knees, holding his hand out.

"What d'ya want, Arthur?"

"The binoculars, man. Quickly."

I handed him the field glasses, and danged if he didn't get down on his belly—right down on his belly in the grass there—and shinny up toward the top of the crest we'd been following.

Well I wasn't going to crawl on my belly for no man, but I did scrunch over and kinda creep up behind him.

The dog—it'd been running beside us all this time as nothing had been said about leaving it behind, and I sure hadn't given any thought to it—looked like it was even more confused than I was. It scrunched down too with its tail low and stayed at my heels.

Arthur got to the top and stopped there. He turned and gave me a smile and held his fingers to his lips for me to be quiet, then he motioned me forward.

I crept up beside him and peered over the top. The herd of antelope was still out there. They hadn't run off when we backed away from where they could see. But some of them looked nervous and plenty wary.

"Sorry, Arthur," I said in a normal tone of voice.

"Shhh!"

"Arthur . . ." I remembered and dropped my voice to a whisper like he wanted, "Arthur, those things're a good quarter mile off. Maybe more. You can't hit 'em way out there."

He wasn't paying attention to me, but was looking first at the antelope and then down at the knobs on the sights of that pretty rifle and then back and forward again.

"Five hundred fifty yards," he whispered.

Looked like a bit more'n a quarter mile to me, but he could call it what he liked.

He fiddled with his sights some more, then stretched out on the ground with his left arm propped sturdy and shoved one of those long cartridges into the breech of the rifle and closed the action, which was of a kind that went up and down, though this wasn't a normal kind of lever-action saddle carbine, and that was for dang sure.

"You're really gonna try and shoot all that way?"

"Shhh."

He leaned down to the sights and held steady, and the next thing I knew, the rifle went off without me noticing his finger move.

There was a puff of smoke and a bellow of noise, and the butt of the thing rocked back against his shoulder. It looked to be a pretty hard push for such a scrawny little fella, but the little Sir never even made a face about it.

I stood up and said, "See. You missed so bad I never even seen dirt fly in front of them."

About that time a big ol' buck antelope on the left side of the bunch jumped up into the air, and when he come down, he just crumpled and fell and lay there. The rest of the herd took off in a belly-down race toward Deadwood and over the next rise.

Arthur gave me a smug kind of look and a wink, but he didn't say anything. He sat up, opened the action of his rifle and removed the empty cartridge. Instead of throwing it away, he dropped the empty into a pocket, not the one holding the other cartridges.

I took another look out across the grass. That buck he'd shot hadn't moved and wasn't going to, it looked like.

"Reckon I should go pack it in," I said. "Fresh meat tonight, eh?"

"Fresh meat, yes, but let me do the skinning. I want to preserve the cape and head for my collection." He brushed off his front and set out toward the distant antelope.

"Don't you want me to ride you over there in the wagon, Arthur? I can bring it down here to get you an' save you the walk."

"Whatever for? Meet me at the carcass, Charles."

For an invalid he sure didn't mind pushing himself. I

reached down to rub the dog's head—it occurred to me now that the dog hadn't been at all upset by the shooting, but then it'd prob'ly been around the end of plenty of coyotes in its time with the sheep herds—and started back toward the wagon.

This Sir was an odd kind of fellow, and that was for dang sure.

When we got back near the wagon, the dog gave a yip and acted like it wanted to race me the rest of the way. I guess I was getting kinda odd myself or something, because damned if I didn't do it, and me and the dog like to have scared those horses outa their harnesses. If I hadn't set those weights, we all would of been afoot.

CHAPTER 11

We went on like that, Arthur stopping now and again to "collect" stuff until the possum belly was groaning from the weight of salted hides and skulls and capes and the inside of the rig was littered with drying samples of flowers and grasses and assorted weeds, and then on the sixth day out of Cheyenne the Sir went an' surprised me.

We'd just been kind of drifting along—or so I'd thought—but now the Sir up and asked, "Tell me, Charles"—I hadn't managed to break him of the habit of calling me that instead of Charlie and had about given up trying—"this stream is a tributary of the Crazy Woman, what?" He had asked me to pull down toward this creek, you see, although our water barrel was about full and it was too early to stop for dinner yet.

"Yeah, I'd say that it about has t' be, running where it does. Yeah, it 'bout has to be."

"The Quail Fork, would you say?"

Now how he would ever have heard of a picayune little crick like the Quail Fork . . .

Well, it wasn't my place to try and worry about that. Just to try and answer him. "Let me give it some thought, Arthur."

I run through in my mind the wanderings we'd been doing, trying to sort out one basin from another and figure which watersheds we'd touched on and what directions we'd gone and about how far.

I mean, this wasn't exactly my home ground. Not that I was unfamiliar with it, but the times I'd been up this way before, I'd generally been going to it or passing through it, like moving beeves up the Bozeman or delivering to this place or that, and not actually working in this part of the country regular, and I had to think on it some before I gave him an answer.

"Prob'ly," I said finally. "Prob'ly the Quail, but I won't swear to it."

The Sir grunted and said, "We'll turn west here, Charles."

"All right." I swung the team wide of the crackwillow and small growth that lined the creek bank and headed them in the direction he wanted. "Something up ahead that I should know about, Arthur?" There wasn't any game or extra-special "collectables" along the bottom here that I could see, although as everyplace else, wherever there was a depression in the ground, like a creek bottom or a gully, there was bones and rotting hides aplenty.

I mean, I'd heard the stories about how bad this past winter had been, but I hadn't really understood it until we got out on the grass north of Cheyenne and could see for ourselves just how bad it had been.

Everyplace where a steer or a cow could try and get out of the wind during a storm there was carcasses piled one on top of the next. Piled so deep that some gullies were filled to the top with cattle that had died in the winter when the first snows were part melted by a break in the weather and melted just enough that when the cold hit again it iced over the grass so that nothing—especially a cow which hasn't sense enough to paw through a crust to get to the snow underneath—could graze and then more storms come in with the whistling winds and temperatures so cold that man nor beast couldn't fight it.

It'd been a terrible winter this winter past, and cows died by the thousands—hell, by the tens of thousands—

and a good many men died too trying to save cows that couldn't be saved.

Anyway, I'd heard it was bad, but I hadn't realized just how bad until we got out to where we could see the dead critters that was left behind.

In early spring the stink must have been terrible and the whole country smelling like a charnel house, but by now the carcasses were mostly dried out. Dismal for any cowman to have to look at, of course, but already falling away back into the earth with wildflowers growing through empty rib cages.

This must have been a helluva fat spring for the coyotes, though.

Anyhow, I held to the south bank of the Quail to avoid the string of carcasses that were piled under the north lip, where the dying cattle had tried to avoid the cut of the wind screaming down from the north, and took us west along the creek.

"Ektually," Arthur said, "I have a stop to make. A visit."

"All right."

His business, not mine. He hadn't said anything about going visiting, but of course it didn't make any nevermind to me. If that was what he wanted to do, he was entitled.

I knew by then, though, that the Sir wasn't any casual visitor at any and all signs of civilization.

I mean, there are some dudes who like to get out and play at roughing it, but you give them a peep at a roof and the first thing they want to do is go and sleep under it. The Sir wasn't like that.

This country wasn't all settled up and crowded, not hardly, but now and then we'd passed within sight of a ranch headquarters or a line shack or a thread of road that looked like it led someplace, and never once had Arthur suggested stopping to meet whoever lived there or to look for a welcome. He'd always preferred to press right ahead an' go on with his own affairs.

So I figured this close-mouthed little invalid Sir had something particular in mind if he wanted to go calling now without a hint of it beforehand. Especially since he'd popped out with the name of Quail Fork when I wouldn't have thought he should ever have heard of a trickle like that that I barely remembered the name of my own self.

He didn't elaborate on it any, though, and I didn't ask. I just kept the wagon pointed in the direction he wanted, and the rest of that drive we didn't stop to inspect nor to collect anything but just kept rolling, even when we saw a black-footed ferret run into a prairie dog's den and might have been able to collect the thing with a little digging and more luck than we'd had the last time he tried to nab one of the creepy little critters. I pointed it out to Arthur, but this time he didn't act at all interested. Just wanted to keep moving.

I thought for a minute there that he might actually have got excited about this visit, whatever it was, but I gave him a good looking over while I scratched the dog's ears and pretended to be looking at it, and the Sir's expression was just as bland and unreadable as it always was. So I guessed I was wrong about that and just kept on driving.

CHAPTER 12

It was a ranch headquarters that we came to, of course, but I mean it was *some* headquarters.

Big? I reckon.

There was a stone house, two stories, that'd already been added to with single story log wings on both sides and another, smaller addition coming out the rear end of the main house. There was a porch or veranda sort of thing built across the whole front of it so that there was a heckuva nice view down the valley of the Quail.

The house was situated at the head of the Quail, at a spring coming out of the low, rolling hills, with a mob of smaller outbuildings set above the spring against the little hill to the north. That was good planning, of course, because by putting them there the whole outfit would be pretty much protected against the north winds and in winter would get the warmth of the sun too. The main house, though, was kind of centered at the head of the valley, below all the other buildings, closer to the spring.

The spring flow had been dammed to create a pond. That was normal enough, of course, except that at this place the pond hadn't been put in as a stock tank but was there to look pretty. Flowers and it looked like maybe even some grass had been planted around the pond, and there were some small trees set out too, and there were white-painted wrought-iron benches and low tables near the trees. Damnedest thing you ever saw when you realized that it was all set out there in the middle of the big grass and not on some swell street in Denver or K.C. or St. Louis. I mean, it looked like a *park*, for cryin' out loud.

It was coming dusk when we got there, and already they had fired up the lamps in the house so that the place looked all bright and gay and lively, even though there wasn't anybody moving around outside that I could see.

There wasn't any lights showing in what I took to be the bunkhouse, but there was a lamp burning in one end of a low building that I guessed was the cookhouse.

I noticed, too, that the corrals—there was a bunch of them strung out downstream from the big barn that was at the lower, east edge of the whole affair—were mostly empty.

Even so, the place looked plenty well tended. Tidy, I guess you would say, right down to the grass that was growing down near the pond. The grass had been cropped close somehow so that it was about all of the same height, short, and looked like a regular town lawn instead of feed for anything.

The main house was stone and dark log, but all the other buildings, and most of them was log too, was all painted white just as pretty as you please.

It was quite a setup to be found out here so far from anything, and I have to say that I was impressed.

There was a road leading off to the south, and we picked it up for the last quarter mile or so before we reached the ranch. Just below the pond there were a pair of stone columns, although with no gate between them nor fence to either side that the road passed through. Over top of those and connecting them was a big old arch sort of deal, made of more wrought iron, and in the center of the curlique design there was a brand worked in iron.

Crown B I would read it as there was a crown shape with a capital B inside it. I didn't recall seeing any cattle wearing the Crown B brand. Although of course most of the cattle we'd seen since leaving Cheyenne were dead, and I hadn't bothered to really look at those. For sure I hadn't seen any live cows carrying that mark.

"Is this the place, Arthur?"

He looked up at the arch with the brand on it and nodded. I still couldn't read his expression, but I thought he was maybe sitting up even straighter now than he usually did. And he always sat straight as if he had a . . . well, he always held himself stiff. Put it that way.

The road curved off toward the ranch buildings, but there was a gravel driveway, like, that went to the front of the big house and made a circle in front of it. I knew without asking that a Sir like Arthur wouldn't be going to the bunkhouse, so I took our house on wheels up the driveway and pulled 'er to a stop in front of the house.

Someone opened the front door and peeped out for a second, then disappeared back inside.

A moment later there was a disturbance at one of the curtains—yes, there was actual curtains at the windows as I could see now that we were close—and then a moment later the front door was flung open and a dark-haired woman came rushing out with her skirts aflying.

Arthur was down off the box of the wagon in a flash, forgetting his cane again, and next thing I knew there was all manner of hugging going on and the woman was crying and the dog was barking at the excitement, and Arthur gave me an embarrassed sort of look over his shoulder while this female hung onto him and bawled.

I didn't know hardly what to do, so I turned my head away and pretended to admire the view down the valley of the Quail.

CHAPTER 13

Now I hadn't wanted to stare, you understand, but it wasn't quite dark yet and I'd got a pretty good look at the woman who'd come running out to greet Arthur and wet down his shirt front.

And I got to say that I was just the least bit envious that it was his shirt that she was hugging up to.

I mean, this gal was a nice looker.

Not plump and apple-cheeked like that Angela back in Cheyenne. In fact she was on the skinny side if anything, built kinda sleek, like a cat, and she was tall too. Not at all what I'd normally think my tastes run to. But there was something about her. In the way she carried herself, even when she was upset like she was. In the way she set her head. In the straight, slim line of her back. Something. I dunno exactly, but whatever it was, she had it. Quality, I guess you'd say.

If things'd been different, I would guess that I'd've been some taken with her myself. But of course Arthur was a Sir and she was what I would say was a lady, the genuine article, and I was just some cowboy hired to drive a wagon.

I expect I thought about that some as I was staring off down the Quail past the tame pond at the spring, and all the while I was listening but trying not to while she was slurping on ol' Arthur.

Neither one of them said all that much, exactly, not that I could hear anyhow, but just from the little I did hear I could tell that this woman, whoever she was, was about as

British as the Sir was, so I guessed they had knowed one another for some while. Not that it was so dang clever of me to figure that out after she'd come running outa the house like she did to see him. But anyway . . .

After a bit the greetings was done, and Arthur got his cane outa the wagon, which told me it was okay to look around again, and the woman went inside to fetch out a Mexican couple, who I guess were housekeepers for her or servants or something. They came out and unloaded the stuff Arthur wanted outa the back.

Meantime the Sir and his ladyfriend was huddled on the porch, him with his arm draped around her waist—mighty slim little bit of a waist it was, too, which mostly I wouldn't find so attractive but somehow on her I did—and her leaning into his shoulder and looking now just as content as a bee in clover.

Soon as his things was unloaded and carried inside, Arthur and the lady disappeared into the house with not a backward look, which I got to say peeved me.

The dog and me was left sitting on the box of the Sir's damned house on wheels without so much as a word. Thanks a helluva lot, Arthur.

Well, it was suppertime and I was hungry and I wasn't going to sit there the whole night waiting to see was the Sir gonna come out or spend the night or what, so I shook the cobs into moving and drove them up beside the cookhouse.

I didn't know what I oughta do for sure, whether to unhitch the team or leave them standing. I settled for leaving them in harness for the time being but pulling their bits and giving them a bait of food, then went into the cookhouse to see what I could find for myself and the dog.

There wasn't anything pushy about that. A man traveling through is welcome to a meal most anywhere I've ever been or heard of, and the Sir for sure acted like he intended staying a while anyhow, what with unloading his things.

I was just in time to get the last of supper from a coosie who sure wasn't overworked from feeding all the hands. There were only two hands in the place and the cook. Three in all for the meal. So there was plenty left over that I could fill myself and give a plate to the dog too.

We didn't talk much—I mean the humans and me—just enough to exchange some names. The cook naturally enough was called Coosie. I didn't even have to ask about that. And the hands were a kid called Kid and a beat-up codger with bad hands and one shoulder carried low from old breaks whose name was Jim. Jim, I expect, was in his late forties. Awful old, anyway, for a man makin' a living on horseback, assuming that he was. For all I knew he might be earning his keep with a hammer and paint brush around the place instead of by swinging a rope. Naturally I didn't want to hurt his feelings by asking. Nobody asked what I was doing there, of course—which was just as well, since I didn't know myself—and I was more interested in the chuck than in conversation, so I ate quick and went back outside.

Didn't look to be any point in keeping the cobs in harness any longer, as by now I could hear the tinkle of music drifting up from the open windows of the main house so that it sounded like Arthur and the lady was having a gay old time of it down there and likely could be expected to keep that up for a spell. So I stripped the harness off the horses and turned them loose in a small pen that had its own pump and trough—I made sure there was plenty of water for them—and set some rocks behind the wagon wheels. I never have learned to trust a brake on a wagon.

After that there wasn't much for it, I figured, except to go to bed, so me and the dog climbed into the back of the wagon to our own bunks for the night.

I would have to say, though, that I was restless for a

while there from thinking about that danged Sir down at the house and the pretty lady he was with. Particularly after the pianna music quit and everything got quiet again. But I gave myself a stern talking to and cuddled up to the dog, and after a bit, I was able to get off to sleep.

CHAPTER 14

I woke up . . . I don't know, midnight maybe . . . to the sounds of some commotion going on down at the big house. I say I woke up. Really it was the dog that woke me. He was whining at the door of the rig and pacing between there and the side of my bunk and acting like he wanted out. It was only after he woke me and got me to sitting up that I heard the noises from down below.

Voices, they were. Loud and becoming angry.

"It's okay," I said, and the dog quieted his fussing.

I pulled my pants on and slid my feet into my boots and tried to remember where I'd put my hat. It was dark in the wagon and I couldn't find the hat for a moment. Then I stepped outside to see what was what.

I could hear the voices a little clearer once I was outside. Most of the lights in the house had been blown out, but the Mexican houseman that I'd seen earlier was on the porch holding a lantern. By its light I could see that there were some riders in the circle driveway just in front of the place. The houseman seemed to be arguing with them about something.

Now like I said before, I know better than to go mixing into other folks's business. I really do. But I was awake and kinda peeved to be that way, and I hadn't anything better to do anyhow. So I drifted down that way.

Besides, I told myself, if they kept this noise up, they were gonna wake the Sir, and an invalid needs all the rest he can get. I told myself that I was just doing right by the fella that paid me.

The Mexican fella was getting excited and louder than ever, but he was losing his English, and the fellas on horseback couldn't understand what he was trying to tell them.

There were four of them I could see when I got close. Four fellas on mighty stout, long-legged horses. I had to admire horseflesh like that and knew that anyone would want to ride for an outfit that mounted its hands on horses so good.

Two of the men, one of them old and the other maybe thirty, was dressed fine, with good coats and collars and fancy boots, even though they were out riding in the middle of the dang night. The other two, who hung their horses back a couple steps, were dressed like any ol' hand except that they were wearing holsters and revolvers on their belts, which most working boys don't bother with, so I guessed they'd all been to town or something—those fellas who do like to own guns and strut around with them don't generally want to be bothered with the things unless they're going someplace special and not just working —and likely now the whole bunch of them was about half shot and not realizing they were bothering people outa their beds.

Having been raised in Texas, I can make out a little Mexican talk. Can't speak it, mind, but I can generally figure out the direction of something being said. What the houseman was saying was that the lady, Doña Elizabeth, was sleeping and he wasn't gonna wake her for these guys at this hour. I can't say that I blamed him neither, as I sure hadn't wanted to wake up.

He was saying all this in Mexican though, loud, and the four riders couldn't understand him and kept hollering back at him even louder that they wanted to see a Mrs. Copperton, who I figured would be the same as the Sir's ladyfriend and the houseman's Doña Elizabeth, and they weren't gonna go without they got to see her.

Well, I went on closer, figuring maybe I could put my

two cents' worth in and get both parties settled. Before I got there, though, one of the riders, the old man who seemed to be in charge of things, got riled and made a motion and the two boys who were his hired hands come off their saddles and onto the porch quick as you please.

They grabbed the houseman one on each side and looked like they were about to do the man some hurt. I mean, those boys did look nasty all of a sudden and for sure not drunk. Not moving that quick, they weren't, so they didn't even have that excuse.

Now I was a guest at this place, I figured, and I didn't want to see a bunch of yahoos start a one-sided brawl that would do no good but disturb everybody. So I up onto the porch right behind them.

I think none of those fellas had likely noticed me coming out of the dark, so the first thing any of 'em knew was when I was standing there right behind them.

And kinda over them too, as neither of those nasty-acting boys was more'n normal size.

I come up onto the porch right behind them just as one of those fellas reached back a fist and would have punched the houseman in the face.

He started to let fly with his punch, and I reached out and took hold of his arm and stopped him from hitting anybody.

He turned around and his eyes got big as he tried to jerk away from my hold on him, but of course I'd been expecting that and he wasn't half strong enough to get the job done. Which did disconcert him considerable, I believe. For a second or two there, I held my arm rigid with him flopping and jerking at the end of it like a trout on a string as he tried to tug loose.

Then his partner reacted to the goings on, and darned if he didn't try and take a swing at me to help out the first one.

Now these boys just didn't have it. They might've been

top hands with cows for all I knew, but they had a bunch
to learn about some other things.

The guy doubled up his fist and tried to hit me, but he
didn't know much about feinting or kicking or really serious scrapping. He just doubled up and let 'er go.

I didn't want to hurt the man—after all, I'd come and
taken them by surprise, and he was only trying to help his
pard—so I snatched his fist with my left hand and hung on
just tight enough to hold him but not to hurt him.

"Now you boys calm down," I whispered. "The man
here is just tryin' to tell you that the lady is sleepin' and he
don't want to wake her. No need to get . . ."

Danged if the guy on my left didn't try and kick me
while I was trying to explain the situation.

I didn't mind that so much but for *where* he was trying
to kick me. I mean, the fair-or-not of polite fighting aside,
there's some things you just naturally don't wanta try with
another guy unless you know dang good and well you can
whip him and get away with it. So this fella kinda got my
goat, and I squoze down pretty hard on the fist of his that I
was holding.

He was still trying to jerk his hand loose from me and
maybe that had something to do with it, so that I squoze
him harder than maybe I should have.

He let out a yelp loud enough to scare a Comanche—a
short one, though, so there was still some hope that it
wouldn't disturb the folks inside—and his eyes rolled back
in his head and he went pale, and his knees collapsed out
from under him in a dead faint.

I guessed that this was a fella who couldn't take much in
the way of hurting. Not that I'd really tried to hurt him,
you understand. I just hadn't had time to *not* hurt him.
Sure stopped him from wanting to kick me, though.

Well, the first guy, the one whose arm I still had hold of,
he decided to get mad about his partner fainting like that.

He quit flopping to try and get loose and acted like he was gonna get serious about being unpleasant.

I didn't want to hurt him too, so I picked him up and carried him down off the porch to where his boss was waiting.

The old man looked kinda disgusted about it all, I thought, for which I couldn't blame him. The young one behind him just looked confused.

"Look," I said in a soft voice that wouldn't carry upstairs, "this whole thing's just a misunderstanding. And it's late and folks are asleep. Why don't you fellas come back tomorra if you want to see the lady o' the house."

I set the cowboy down beside his boss and turned loose of him, and the fool was so upset he made a grab for the gun he was wearing on his belt.

He was just upset. I knew that. Still it was a stupid thing for him to do when we were standing there belly to belly like that. I took the gun away from him and stuffed it into my back pocket, and this one looked pale too, though I hadn't done anything to hurt him.

"Dan. Let it be," the old man said in a sharp voice.

Just that quick, Dan got over looking angry and settled down polite as you please.

"Do you want me to go up t' the bunkhouse and see could they put you up for the night?" I asked in a whisper, trying to remind the old man that it was the middle of the night.

He gave me a cold-eyed look and didn't say anything, so I took it that he didn't want the help.

Over on the porch, the fella who'd passed out on us was coming around again. I went up, and me and the house-man helped him onto his feet, and I took him by the arm and helped him down to his horse.

"Come back tomorra, fellas," I suggested.

"You tell that . . ." well, I won't repeat what the man said, but it wasn't nice, ". . . tell her that I'll be back."

"I'll be glad to do that." I was gonna ask who I should say had called, but before I could, the old man wheeled his horse around and threw the steel to it, the other three going right with him, and the four riders took off down the valley.

I felt something wet on my hand and looked down, and there the dog was with its tail held low and a whine in its throat.

"It's all right now," I said and leaned down to scratch it behind the ears.

The houseman came and thanked me, still so excited that he was still talking Mexican, but I could understand pretty much what he was saying.

"De nada," I told him.

Me and the dog started back up toward the wagon, and it was only then that I noticed that those fellas had gone and woke up the Sir after all.

Arthur was standing just inside the curtains of one of the windows with the lady beside him hanging onto his arm like she'd been trying to stop him from coming out. I was glad she'd done that but was sorry that he had been woke up after all.

I pretended not to see them as that might be embarrassing to them both and went on back to my bed.

CHAPTER 15

I woke the next morning later than usual, past sunup, and saw that blued steel revolver laying there on the stove and for a moment forgot what a thing like that was doing there. Then I remembered. I'd taken the thing from that Dan last night and had forgot to give it back to him before they rode off.

No harm done, I figured. They'd said they'd be back. I could give it to him then.

I yawned and stretched and let the dog out for his morning business, then got dressed and found the backhouse. By then Coosie had hollered that breakfast was ready—there was an iron triangle hanging beside the cookhouse door, but I guess with so few hands on the place as there seemed to be here, he didn't think there was any point in using the thing—so I washed and went inside to eat.

Coosie already had a plate out for me, and the Kid was there already stuffing his face hard and fast like he couldn't get enough. The gimped-up cowboy named Jim came in just behind me.

"This is awful good," I said. "Sure beats trying to put up with my own cookin'." It never hurts to be on the good side of a cook.

"Thanks."

"You boys didn't hear none of the racket last night?"

"Racket? What racket?"

"Bunch of riders come in during the night and wanted

the lady woke up for something. They went away after a spell."

"What'd they look like?" Coosie asked.

I told him.

"That sonuvabitch Harper," Jim said.

The Kid, he just kept eating, but he did cut his eyes toward Jim with a worried sort of look.

"He didn't cause any trouble?" Coosie asked. His tone of voice and what Jim had just said made it sound like trouble might be expected out of this man named Harper.

"Naw. Nobody wants trouble in the middle of the night."

"That SOB would," Coosie said.

"If you say so." I helped myself to another plate of hoe cakes and sowbelly. "You boys sure eat good here."

"What did Harper want?"

"He never said. Just that he'd be back." I poured syrup over the hoecakes and tried them. The second plate of them was as good as the first had been.

"That sonuvabitch," Jim said again.

Coosie gave Jim a dark look.

"Don't worry," Jim said. "I got it oiled up."

"Sounds like you're talkin' about a gun," I said.

"Ayuh. An' I'll use it too if I have to." Jim pushed his plate away with his meal half eaten. He looked like maybe he was too upset to have much of an appetite after what I'd told them.

I wanted to ask what the trouble was, but I wasn't any part of the Crown B and didn't want them to think I was nosing in where I didn't belong. After all, I was just passing through. They belonged here.

The Kid looked uncomfortable. Didn't quit eating, though. It was a marvel that anybody so scrawny could hold so much.

Jim built himself a cigarette and smoked it before he

left the table, but he never went back to his meal. I hurried up and finished and went out behind him.

"Be glad to help with the chores," I told him.

"Not that much to do, but I thank you for the offer."

"Well, whatever there is, I'd be pleased to help with it."

I trailed him over to the barn. There were a few horses in there, lightweight fancy stock with coats so slick and shiny they looked like they'd been oiled. Out in the corral nearest the barn there were a few head of working stock a cut or more above average. Judging from what I'd seen so far, there was some awful fine horseflesh in this part of the country.

I noticed that in addition to that one shoulder that dropped, Jim limped some on that side when he walked. I said, "I'll climb up in the loft an' fork some hay down if you like."

"Don't bother," he said. "No hay up there."

"No?" It was an awful big loft. You would think they could put enough hay up there to winter over twenty times the horses I'd seen on the place.

"Nope," Jim said.

I took another skeptical look overhead.

"Fed it all last winter," Jim said, picking up a gallon pail. "The boss, he tried to haul hay out t' the cattle. Wasn't enough of it to make a spit in the bucket. He knowed that, o' course, e'en before we tried to tell 'im. But he figured he had to try an' save them. Never come close, an' because of it we lost some horses t' winterkill too."

I grunted. What can you say to something like that. It'd been a tough situation, I guessed.

I'd never heard of anybody trying to hay-feed cattle through a winter, though. You just always figured on a winter loss of maybe five percent. But that was always more than made up by your spring birthings, which were generally figured to make an overall herd increase of twenty percent even after losing your winter-killed stock.

That's the way the cow business had always been, long as I could remember, and I'm sure for a lot longer.

This last winter up here hadn't been like anything that came before it though. I had to wonder if having hay enough on hand to winter-feed the cattle too would've made a difference in the survival rate. Not that I could understand anybody ever being able to put up enough hay to do that.

Hell, how much hay would it take to feed a cow through a winter? A ton? Two? Far as I knew, nobody'd ever had reason to ask that question. A damn sure bunch of it, that much I was sure. And for the big boys with herds of ten, twenty thousand head . . . why, hay enough to feed that many bovines was just more than my brain could handle. It'd take haystacks built like mountains to get that job done.

Jim lifted the lid off a barrel and began to scoop grain out into buckets. Lots of grain. Without hay to feed he was giving the horses grain. No wonder they looked so sleek and fat. They were eating groceries just about as expensive as what the humans ate around here.

Jim saw me looking at him and explained, "There's a trap under fence out back. I'll turn 'em onto that this afternoon to let 'em get some grass. Gotta put more in their bellies than grain."

"Uh huh. Nothing I can do to help?"

"Nope."

"Then I'll go see to the wagon horses."

"Here." He scooped me two gallons of grain into a bucket and handed it to me for the cobs.

"Thanks." I went back out into the bright, morning sunshine to tend to my own business while Jim took care of his. The Kid was finally leaving the cookhouse about the time I got done with that chore.

CHAPTER 16

"Good morning, Charlie," Arthur said, sounding about half embarrassed when he said it.

I guess I gaped at him. I mean, he hadn't called me Charlie, always Charles, practically since I'd met him, him being generally so formal. Now here he'd gone and said it all on his own. Sounded like it tasted funny in his mouth, of course, but he'd said it.

He'd come up the hill, carrying his cane but not using it much, while I was propped up on a log section not split yet and leaning against the side of the barn in the sunshine. I'd been whittling, not paying attention much to what else was going on, so I hadn't seen him coming or would have gone down to meet him and saved him the trouble of the walk.

"Mornin', Arthur." I stood up and dropped my whittle-stick and shoved my knife back into my pocket.

"About last night . . ." he began.

Now I knew he was gonna go to thanking me, so I cut him off short. "I'm sorry them fellas woke you, Arthur, but there wasn't no harm done, I expect. I'd ruther not talk about it any more if it's all the same to you."

He gave me an odd kinda look but nodded, agreeing that that was all right with him if that's what I wanted.

For just a second there he looked like he wanted to say something more but didn't and after a moment said, "Lady Copperton and I should like to take a drive today. Would you drive us please, Charlie?" He was nice enough to put it like a question even though it wasn't.

"Sure thing," I said. "You want me to hitch up the house for you?" What I was thinking, though, was that he'd said 'Lady' Copperton. Shee-oot, she *was* the gen-u-wine thing. A real Lady just like ol' Arthur was an actual Sir. Shee-oot. I guessed I hadn't been surrounded by so much quality since the time I'd got drunk unexpected and stumbled into the Cattleman's Club down in Fort Worth one time.

Arthur shook his head and said, "No, I understand there should be a more suitable vehicle available. Ask one of the . . ." he hesitated, ". . . hands?" I nodded. "Ask one of the hands to show you where."

"I c'n do that."

He nodded and traipsed off down toward the house again.

I glanced up toward the sun. It was maybe eight, eight-thirty and looked to be a nice day for a drive. I have to admit that I was some envious of the Sir for being the one doing the riding with the lady—Lady, I mean—while I was up front doing the driving an' having to pretend not to see nor hear anything behind me.

Still, a job is a job an' I've never been a shirker. I take some pride in that and wasn't gonna start changing my ways now.

I picked up the whittling stick I'd been playing with and dropped it in my pocket as those can be scarce in the big grass country sometimes and went off to look for Jim. I couldn't find him, but the Kid showed me a whole collection of dandy rigs stored in one of the outbuildings.

"Miz Copperton likes this one," he said, pointing to a real spanker of an outfit. It was a phaeton, an actual, honest-to-pete phaeton, way out here in the middle of nothing, with a fold-down top that could be put up over the passenger seat but leave the driver stuck out front in the open. The thing was painted and polished to a fare-thee-well and the spokes of the wheels painted bright yellow and even them polished too. I mean it was *some*, it was. Damn flimsy for rough country, of course, but awful pretty.

While I pulled it out of the shed and collected the fancy harness for it off the wall behind where it'd been parked, the Kid went and found the team that Mrs. Copperton favored, which turned out to be a pair of sleek long-barrelled sorrels that looked like enough to be the same horse twice.

The Kid helped me hitch them in the unfamiliar harness, and I drove them down to the front of the house, finding that they worked as pretty as they looked and shouldn't be any trouble to handle.

When I got there, danged if the Mexican houseman didn't come out hauling a great huge wicker basket that he strapped onto the back of the phaeton.

"Dinner," he explained, his English back now that it was daylight and he wasn't excited anymore. He leant close to my ear and whispered, "Your dinner is in the box, *señor*. For you som'ting special, eh?" He grinned at me and winked. An' that, you see, is the kind of thank-you I can get along with. I thanked him right back, and he went off inside the house.

Directly the Sir an' Lady Elizabeth Copperton come out, laughing and acting gay an' happy, and for the Sir's sake I put on my politest, helpfulest look an' off we all went for a picnic in the sunshine. And I didn't look around nor stare at the lady even once.

CHAPTER 17

The "som'ting special" in my dinner box turned out to be a huge slab of dried apple pie, which is one of my very special favorites, as I guess it is for most ol' boys who've spent any time on the cow trails. I did appreciate it.

The Sir and the Lady had sure found themselves a dandy place for their picnic, I got to say.

Like so much good grazing ground, this country could be awful shy of water, but Mrs. Copperton directed the way to a pocket ten, twelve miles from the headquarters where a seep had caused a pond down in the bottom of it and a part-time creek bed that was already dry for the rest of the year. The seep seemed to be year-round though, as there were some fine old trees growing there and a tangle of wild plum and gooseberry and currants on what would sometimes be the downstream edge of the copse. It was fine, all right, and just the place for privacy if that was what you wanted.

Funny thing about that, though. The whole morning's drive the Sir and the Lady had talked, of course, but it all sounded more friendly than, um, *friendly*. If you know what I mean.

I mean, I wasn't eavesdropping. Exactly. But I couldn't shut my ears off, even if I was careful not to look around at them. And their talk was all pretty ordinary. Most of it about cows and grass and the country we was driving through—and I got to say that the lady—Lady—knew what she was saying right well. She was a better judge of grass than a lot of men I've known, including a lot of men who, if you asked them, would make out that they knew it all, even though *no*body knows it all, and what she said about grazing prospects were just about what I'd've said my own self. I was impressed by that, let me tell you.

Anyway, the whole morning they hadn't got to billing and cooing or playing smacky-face that I could hear. Which kind of surprised me a little, but which I did kinda appreciate in a way.

I mean, I'd gotten a pretty fair look at the Lady the last night, but now in broad daylight I got an even better one. And she was even prettier than I'd thought, and I had thought her awful pretty to begin with.

She had dark brown hair, which I'd already known, but in the sunlight it showed glints of red in it. And her eyes were . . . I don't really know exactly what to call that color. Not blue exactly nor green either. Somewhere in between. I've seen flowers that color, but I don't know what those would be called. Big eyes, anyhow, and the color running so deep an' true a fella could swim in them.

When she'd come out to the phaeton and I'd helped her into it that morning, I think I'd been rude enough to stare a little when I looked into those eyes. And I was certainly wrong to think so, but for just a bit there, I'd almost believed that she blinked and stared back for just a second or two. Caught her breath, sort of. I don't know. Stupid of me to think that, of course. Still, the plain fact was that I was dang well taken by her and knew I wouldn't be sleeping so good until Arthur quit his visiting and we could get back to collecting stupid stuff to drag along in the wagon.

One of the things that I'd noticed—not that she had commented on it, but I'd heard—was that we hadn't passed a living critter the whole ten or twelve miles except for wild things like antelope—which they were far as I was concerned, no matter what the Sir said—and prairie dogs and stuff like that.

Not a horse nor a cow nor a sheep. Noplace. And in cow-raising country you have to find that kinda remarkable.

Beside the seep where we stopped for lunch there was a spread of light, sandy gravel. There wasn't a track in it, save for the tiny-wee little hoofprints left by antelope and some bird tracks and light scratchings that could've been left by any of the little things like rabbits or foxes or whatever. But not a single horse or cow track.

I'd carried the big basket down beside a fallen log in a shady spot and helped Arthur lay out their lunch spread, most of which come in tins or boxes and was stuff I couldn't recognize, even after I read the labels, and then carried my separate packed lunch pail off to the other side of the grove without waiting to be asked. I kinda missed the dog, which had been left back at the house with the wagon.

After I ate, I sure didn't want to bother Arthur and the Lady, so I wandered down to the plum thicket to see if any fruit was set, even though I knew perfectly well that it was much too early for anything to be coming ripe. The thicket wouldn't offer any dessert, which I didn't need anyhow after that fine piece of pie, but it was thick and private and I wanted to take a leak out of sight.

I was in there, outa sight, when those same four riders from the night before come loping over the rise and down to the phaeton. Harper, the boys back at the ranch had called their bossman.

I liked the looks of them even less in daylight than I had the night before, and I kind of hung in the thicket where I was instead of rushing out to see what was gonna happen.

CHAPTER 18

Last night, with the houseman, Harper had been hard and cold and arrogant. I don't like people who're arrogant. It says about them that they think they're better than other folks, and I don't guess that is up to them to decide.

Today the old man—he was in his fifties, maybe sixties, I thought—was hard and cold but not so arrogant. He acted different when he was talking to the Sir and the Lady than he'd been when it was an excited Mex servant in front of him. Not polite exactly but keeping a closer rein on himself.

He stopped his horse, the nice-dressed younger man beside him, and like before the two boys backing him up stayed a few steps behind.

"Mrs. Copperton." His voice was as hard as the set of his jaw. He nodded but didn't touch his hat brim.

"Mr. Harper." I would have to say that her voice was just as cold as his. But then I'd gathered from what Jim said this morning that there was bad feeling between them. Harper was no stranger to the Crown B.

Harper opened his mouth to say something, but she beat him to it. "Arthur, this is the . . . gentleman," the tiny pause there said that she was stretching the point for the sake of politeness, "I was telling you about last night. Justin Harper."

The look Arthur gave that Harper damn sure wasn't a friendly one.

"Mr. Harper, this is Arthur Cooke-Williams. *Sir* Ar-

thur." Her chin rose a little and firmed, like with pride or
defiance. "My brother."

Harper, he glanced at Arthur but didn't howdy him,
which of course was just plain rude.

And me, I was thinking at that moment not so much
about Justin Harper and whatever problems the Crown B
was having but about that pretty little gal saying that the
Sir was her *brother.*

Boy, had I got *that* one figured wrong.

Shee-oot. Danged if that didn't swell my chest an' get
me to grinning. Ol' Arthur was the Lady's brother. Shee-
oot!

Harper was saying something else now, and I'd missed
the first bit of it, whatever it was, but it wasn't nice. What I
finally caught onto was ". . . last time, Mrs. Copperton. I
have already spoken with the executor of your husband's
estate, and he informs me . . ."

I lost the thread of the conversation there, getting off on
thinking that Jim had said something this morning about a
boss at the place and how that person must've been the
Lady's husband and how now it was looking like the husband was dead, prob'ly one of those who got caught in the
die-up trying to save his cows and died with them and
how that meant that the Lady was a widow-woman and
how . . . You get the idea. I was off an' ruminating when
I should've been paying attention.

Time I got to paying attention again and looked up,
Harper must've said something else, something that Arthur didn't like, for the Sir was red in the face and march-
ing toward Harper all stiff-legged and stiff-backed.

"What you require, sir, is a sound caning," Arthur de-
clared, and he looked like he was fixing to take on the
chore. He marched straight at Harper's horse with his
cane raised and looked like he was about to haul Justin
Harper outa the saddle and whup him.

Of course a whip-thin invalid like the Sir wasn't gonna

be able to get a thing like that done, even if he was left to try his dangedest. I mean, Harper was an older fella, but he looked in good enough shape to defend himself from a little guy like Arthur.

Harper must not have seen it that way or something, because just like last night he didn't do for himself but left it to his hired hands to tend to. He turned and said something to the one called Dan and it was Dan who come out of the saddle and went at Arthur with his fists balled for a fight.

Now I couldn't hardly stand there and let the Sir get whipped by that hardcase Dan, so I stepped out of the thicket and started for them.

They were some distance away from the bushes where I'd been, and before I could get there, I wasn't actually needed to deal with ol' Dan.

Dan balled his fists and came on in a rush, looking as ornery as a brown bear fixing to give what-for to a yappy poodle dog. He looked purely mean, in fact, and if I'd been as little as the Sir and in his place, I expect I'd've been scared.

If the Sir was scared, he didn't show it much. Dan came barrelling in on him, and slick as you please, the Sir's cane darts out and bops Dan over his ear and then zips down and tangles in Dan's legs, and then next thing you know old Dan's down on the ground wondering how he got there and why there's a gash pouring blood out the side of his head.

He come to his hands and knees and shook his head like an old bull that's lost a contest with the new herd leader, and blood spattered off to the sides and freckled the Sir's shiny boots red.

About that time the other fella, whose name I hadn't heard, goes to jump down off his horse to help Dan take care of one scrawny Sir, but by that time I was close, so I moved over to the other side of his horse, coming up on the offside of the animal just about the time he wants to step off the near side.

I reached over and took hold of his belt and hauled him across his own saddle to my side of the horse and kinda held him there and grinned at him. "One at a time," I told him, "or it wouldn't hardly be fair."

He cussed me and threw a punch which landed on my shoulder and didn't hurt at all. Didn't hurt me, anyhow. He let out a beller like it hurt him plenty, and it was then that I remembered that I'd already done some damage to this same fella's hand and must have broke something last night or at least got him awful tender to be hitting on people with that fist.

For safety's sake I pulled the guy's gun out of his holster and pushed it down into my own waistband before I dropped him and paid attention to the things that was still going on elsewhere.

I guess Dan must've made another rush at Arthur, for now he was down on his knees a little ways away from where he'd been before and there was blood coming down the other side of his face too.

Arthur was standing there looking calm and as cool as the inside of an ice house and leaning on his cane. Dan was welted and bleeding in two places, and Arthur hadn't mussed his cravat. I thought that was kinda funny and awful good for an invalid to manage.

Dan didn't seem to think it was so funny, of course, and neither did the guy who was lying by my feet. But that one looked up and saw me peering down at him and decided not to mix into it any more.

The young fella who was with Harper swung a leg over his cantle, but Harper stopped him.

"Enough," Harper snapped. "This isn't what we came here for."

Arthur nodded, apparently satisfied that he got to cane one of them even if it wasn't Harper himself, and the young fella sat back down in his saddle and the other two picked themselves up and brushed off and limped back to their horses.

"It would be to your advantage to reconsider," Harper said, looking at the Lady.

She gave him a fiery look but not the satisfaction of an answer. Just a lift of her chin and a glare, which was for sure enough to say everything that she wanted said.

"On your head it is then, madam."

Harper wheeled his horse around and looked like he was ready for a dust-raising exit, but he had to wait while Dan quit dabbing at his head with his kerchief and crawled onto his horse.

Then they threw the spurs to their horses and took off with the gravel flying.

I was half expecting the one I'd tussled with to try and ride me over with his horse when they went, but the guy took a look and saw that I was ready for him, ready to have me a handful of bridle and bring horse an' rider both down to their knees, and at the last second he veered wide and rode around with some muttering and cussing.

"Hell, Arthur," I said. "That was kinda fun."

He gave me a thin-lipped hint of a smile under that stiff little mustache of his and turned to go see to his sister.

"Beggin' your pardon, ma'am," I added.

She laughed and clapped her hands and said, "But I agree with you. Truly I do. Why, I haven't had so much fun since . . ." Her pretty face lost its animation and she looked sad. "Since Edward died," she finished lamely.

"You folks ready for me to tidy up now?" I asked, figuring they needed a change of subject after that one.

Arthur took the Lady by the arm and walked her down toward the pond, and I set in to clean up the picnic things and put it all back into the basket.

CHAPTER 19

Mrs. Copperton came trailing over toward the phaeton, the Sir a step or two behind, and I went to help her into the thing, but instead she smiled and stuck her hand out.

"Arthur is a dear, you know, but quite stuffy. We haven't been properly introduced, and this is twice now that I, we, owe you thanks." She was still smiling. Lordy but did she look pretty when she done that.

I began to stammer something, then remembered to snatch my hat off, and pushed my own big paw out, careful not to take hold of her too hard. "Uh, Charlie, ma'am. Charlie Roy."

Her smile got brighter. "Yes. Quite. And I am Elizabeth Copperton."

Behind her I could see that the Sir was feeling a tad uncomfortable at the idea that his high-born sister would be so easy with the help. Which was me. He didn't *say* anything, but I could see it.

"Thank you, Charlie, for helping us. Those men . . ." She made a face and shrugged. "They are most unpleasant."

"Yes, ma'am."

"But you were so *strong,* Charlie. Gracious, I don't believe I've ever . . ." Danged if she didn't reach up an' give my arm a squeeze on the muscle.

"Yes, ma'am," I said again. It was all I could think of, though there wasn't no point to it. I could feel my face getting hot and hoped she couldn't see. I mean, this was one *good*-looking woman. An' her brother was standing there looking an' not liking it.

Still smiling, her expression not changing a lick, she turned to look at Arthur but asked me, "What do you think about the pasturage here, Charlie? You know livestock, don't you? I've been trying to tell Arthur over lunch that we can come back from the setbacks of this past winter. What do you think?"

The Sir scowled, and I wasn't sure just what I ought to say, so I stuck with the truth.

"Well, ma'am . . ."

"Elizabeth," she corrected.

"Yes, ma'am. Elizabeth. Well, Mrs. Copperton, I wasn't wanting to overhear or nothing, but I heard you talkin' some on the way out, y' know. And I guess I'd have to agree with what you said then. The grass's good. That's for sure. Only thing wrong with it is that there ain't anything left to eat it."

"See!" she told her brother, like that solved something.

The Sir, he scowled again. He looked like he wanted to say something, but glanced at me and didn't.

Now I didn't want to get mixed into a family fuss between these two and that was for sure. I was glad when Arthur changed the subject. "Has the team been watered, Charles?"

"Sure have," I told him.

"I suggest we return now," Arthur said to his sister.

She gave Arthur a sweet smile, the kind that was just a tad *too* sweet, if you know what I mean, and that says that this subject was put off for a bit but dang sure not closed, an' then she gave me an odd sort o' smile an' hopped up into the phaeton before I could move to help her. Arthur followed, not much of anything showing on his face.

I took one more quick look around to make sure nothing had been forgot where they'd had their picnic and then I crawled up onto the box and headed the rig back toward the Crown B.

CHAPTER 20

"So what's the deal with this Harper fella?" I asked in the cookhouse after supper. I pushed my plate back and refused Jim's offer of a chew.

"That sonuvabitch," Jim said.

"Bastard," the Kid added around a mouthful of thirds or fourths.

"We don't like him," Coosie said.

"I kinda guessed that much," I told him. "But how come?"

"Harper's big cheese in this country," Coosie said.

"Got the only place between Cheyenne an' the Yellowstone bigger'n the Crown B," Jim added.

"The bee in his bonnet's that Ed Copperton came into this country just about as early as Harper did. Fact is, the two of them were friends back then."

"This was before the Indian troubles was ended, y' understand. Before it was real safe for anybody t' be takin' up grazing land here."

"The two of 'em stood together then, one outfit supportin' the other if it looked like trouble, and both of 'em taking up claims on the water holes. You know how that is."

I nodded. Indeed I did know. The big cow outfits, the way they'd work things in country where there was more grass than water, they'd file land claims on ground just big enough to hold their headquarters and then separate claims wherever there was steady water to be found. Because in country like this, if you own two water holes, you also as good as own every speck of grass between them two water holes.

There's no way anybody could hope to hold title to all his grass anyhow. A Homestead Act claim, that only gives each man—or woman or kid or whatever, because women are entitled to claims too and there's ways to shuffle the deck so a kid can take title to a claim too—anyway, each of them only gives each person a hundred sixty acres, a quarter section, of free ground.

Now to some fella back east like in Ioway or Ohio or such places, I understand that a quarter section parcel like that sounds like an awful lot. And I expect it would be for somebody intending to farm it and have to follow the south end of a mule back and forth over it for the rest of his natural life.

But when you're talking grazing instead of farming, a quarter section of ground isn't but a spit in a bucket to what's really needed.

This country right where the Crown B was, you could figure forty, forty-five acres would feed one cow. I've known a lot o' grazing ground where it would take a whole quarter section Homestead grant to make a living for one cow.

Say right here, though, and figure it at forty acres for a cow. That's four head grazing on the whole Homestead grant. A man don't make much of a living off a four-head herd, and that is a fact.

Of course, the Homestead grants, those are just the most popular ways to get title to free ground. There's others too. The Timber Act—which is what those folks back in Washington call it an' allow it as, even though there's places here where you can go forty mile between trees—that provides for more land, and then there's some other ones too, I think. Any big cowman could tell you because he's sure to have used them all.

But all told, if you filed for titled land under each an'

every one of those grant acts, a fella couldn't get land enough to graze a herd half big enough to support a family. And at that, it'd have to be a family that didn't eat much nor wear out many shoes.

So the way it really works, a fella wanting to start him a place, he will file on a headquarters location and then he will file again on forty acres here where there's a seep and eighty acres there where there's a pond and a long, skinny, stretched-out quarter section someplace else, laid out maybe only a hundred yards wide, but stretching from here to Glory where there's a creek. And he'll keep that sort o' thing up, claiming water and therefore getting the use of all the grass around it, until he's run out of legal ways he can file claims.

Doing it that way he can run up a respectable sized outfit that maybe only owns two, three thousand acres of ground but that really covers sixty, eighty square miles of grazing country.

Now that prob'ly sounds like a lot, but in cow country it really isn't. It's big enough to carry a nice herd, but not to get rich off of.

The really big boys, them as are in the business in a big way and want to make profits for investors like those rich Englishmen I mistook Arthur to be, they need grazing lands that run into the *hundreds* of square miles. I mean, we're talkin' *big* here.

So what they'll do after they run out of the regular government grant ways a fella can lay claim to water, they'll get their hands to file land claims and prove up on them and then the outfit will buy the claim off the cowboy. Or truth to tell, they'll get the cowboy to make his claim and then everybody pretend it's proved up and go ahead and make the sale without waiting, which you can do more or less legal if you pay a fee to shorten the prove-up time.

I've filed three Homestead claims myself and once a

Timber Act claim and passed the land along to whatever
fella I was working for at the time, and I've sure never
stayed in one spot long enough to prove up on any kind of
grant title. The hands don't mind as there's always a bonus
in it for the cowboy. Twenty dollars is about the going
rate, and for the Timber claim I filed I got fifty dollars. The
government don't seem to mind it neither, as I'm sure
there is no way they could not know what's being done
with their eastern-written Acts.

Anyhow, yeah, I sure did know what Jim and Coosie
were talking about. The cow business. That's all.

"But then there was something happened," Coosie said.
"I don't know what it coulda been. But after that, Harper
and Ed wasn't friendly any more. They wasn't enemies,
mind, but they weren't friendly neither."

"It hung like that," Jim said, "till this past winter. Would
of stayed the same right along, I guess, except that Ed got
himself killed."

"Froze?" I asked.

"Ayuh. Stiff as a fence post by the time the boys found
him. They said he'd come off his horse somehow, likely it
slipped an' fell with him, and he bonked his head on
something an' had been tryin' to crawl home when he
went under. The horse come back without him, o' course,
which is why there was a bunch of us out looking for him."

I raised an eyebrow and looked around the big table
with only the four of us sitting at it. "A bunch?"

"There was a full winter's crew on at the time. Six of us
plus Coosie here at the main place an' three line camps
manned. But that was when we had a whole herd of critters to watch out for, you understand. Hell, there was a
couple dozen of us on the place last summer, an' at that
we had our hands full keepin' up with everything that
needed doing."

That made sense. Now that there wasn't any cows,

there wasn't much need for cowboys. I nodded, and Jim went on.

"Anyhow," he said, "Ed froze and the cattle froze, and now this sonuvabitch Harper is pushing Miz Elizabeth to try and get control of Ed's place and take it out from under her."

"Harper still has cows?"

"Some. There was a few made it through by hiding from the wind under some buttes on his ground. And I hear he's been bringing more in lately, though Lord knows what he'd have to be paying to get them."

I grunted. Jim would be damn sure right about that. With so many cows dead in this part of the country, the fellas down south were getting top dollar and then some for whatever they wanted to sell north. It was just that sort o' deal that had brought me up this year with John Hanks and his herd of stockers to repopulate that Bosler fella's place.

"He's got big plans, Harper has, and he wants the water claims from the Crown B. Word is that he's got a big gov'ment contract to supply beef to the Crow Agency and the North Cheyenne and some say to Pine Ridge too. Even though he hasn't got steers enough on his grass right now to feed a lodge o' Diggers."

"He ain't thinking short term," Coosie said. "That contract's supposed to be for five years and likely renewable. My thinking is that he could make out fat in the long run, even if he had to buy steers outside and sell them at a loss to get through this year's deliveries and the next. If he has cash enough to carry over."

"What we know for sure," Jim said, "is that the sonuvabitch has been pushing Miz Elizabeth to try and give up the Crown B."

"Which she don't want to do," Coosie added.

"Not that she's in shape to hold him off if it comes to money," Jim said.

"Ed didn't leave her all that well fixed, I guess."

"About everything that man could put together was plowed into this place."

"He was upgradin' like hell. Always wantin' to upgrade. Everything he could get was put into upgradin'," Coosie said.

"Brought in a bunch of purebred white-face bulls. Even some damn white-face cows, if you can believe that. O' course not a one of them sons o' bitches made it through the winter. Not a single bull that I know of. Maybe a handful of the cows."

Coosie smiled without much humor. "A couple young steers made it. We're eating a long yearling white-face now."

"It don't taste any better to me," I said, and I guess I sounded a tad grumpy when I said it. The truth is, white-faces are something of a peeve of mine. The damn things just aren't my notion of what a cow oughta be. Nothing wrong with good old Texas range cattle that I've ever seen. Those longhorned SOBs can fight off anything up to an' including bears and make a living where a horny toad would starve, and their cows drop calves as easy as squirting a watermelon seed.

"Likely there wouldn't have been half so much winter kill if he'd stuck to regular cattle," I said.

"You could be right," Coosie said, "but I got to admit that when you butcher there's a difference, an' the white-face is the better. More meat on 'em."

"Well, I expect if you like them so much you can comb the cutbanks all around here and pick up all the white-face meat you want these days." I didn't sound real pleasant about it, I guess.

Coosie held his hands up, palms forward, and smiled. "Hey, I'm not wanting a fuss about it. Just telling you what happened."

I smiled back at him. "Sorry."

"Ed was a good man," Jim said. "He was only doing what he thought was right."

"I suppose. Pity his widow has to pay for it now, though," I said, coming back to the original point.

"She's a nice lady," the Kid put in. He had finally got done eating sometime in the past few minutes. I hadn't been sure that was possible.

I pushed my chair back and stood, my joints creaking and popping some when I did. "Thanks for the meal."

"I got some scraps for the dog," Coosie said. "Wait a second and I'll get 'em."

I thanked him again and carried the stuff outside to where the dog was waiting, still acting like he'd actually missed me today. Danged if I could get over that.

CHAPTER 21

I didn't see the Sir much that next day. He came up to the barn early and saddled a horse and rode off somewhere to the north without saying more than hello and good-bye. I tried to make myself useful while he was gone. Cleaned and straightened up the inside of the house on wheels. Rubbed the harness down with oil and resewed a place where the threads were worn. Played with the dog some. Like that.

After dinner the lady came up to the barn where I was doing some casual whittling. "Could you help me with something, Charlie?"

"You bet," I said, though her own hands were right close by somewhere too. I closed my pocket knife and put it away and followed her down to the big house.

I hadn't been inside the big house before. Whee-ew it was grand. I mean, this place was fitted out nicer than the Cattleman's Club. Or anyplace.

Fancy curtains at all the windows. Fancy carpet on all the floors. Wallpaper patterned with soft, fuzzy stuff, whatever you call that. I'd seen it once before and know there is a special name for it, but I don't recall what that name would be.

Furniture? Lordy! The stuff was all big and soft and looked so deep a fellow could sink into it and get lost down in there. I didn't try and sit on any of it, as I didn't know what the state of the backside of my jeans might be. But I sure was tempted, just to see how something like that might feel.

The walls was all full of mirrors and pictures and lamps on sconces—that word is right; I remember that'n for some reason—and the ceilings hung with fancy candelabra things—except I think you call those something else when they're hanging from a ceiling—that were oil lamps and not just candle holders. The lights had teardrop-shaped things dangling from them that looked like diamonds except they weren't. At least I don't *think* they were.

She led me in through a vestibule and a foyer that was big enough to hold a piano and *did* and off into a huge parlor and then back through that into a man-looking study sort of room. That one was different from the others because, instead of wallpaper, it had polished wood paneling on the walls and a big old fireplace with deer and elk horns mounted over the mantle. And if you've ever seen a good elk rack, and this was a good one for sure, you know how tall the ceilings must've been to allow for such a thing to be put over top of the mantle. There was a gun rack against one wall and a pair of leather-covered chairs facing the fireplace with a game table and chess board set between the chairs and . . . well, it was some, that's what it was. It was just some.

The lady smiled at me and stopped beside a rolltop desk that would've been too big to fit into most rooms but seemed almost small in this one.

"What do you think, Charlie?"

"About what, ma'am?"

"This room. Do you like it?"

"Yes, ma'am." I mean, what the hell *could* I say. Sure I liked it. Anybody would.

She ran her fingertips over the front of the desk and looked like she was studying the grain of the wood or passing judgment on the polishing job that the houseman had done or something. She wasn't looking at me, anyhow. "This was my husband's retreat," she said. "He always said a man should have a place of his own. Do you agree, Charlie?"

I couldn't help myself. I tipped my head back and laughed out loud, her thinking about her dead husband or not. "Ma'am," I told her, "your brother might be able to give you an answer to that one. Me, I figure I'm doing all right if I got a bedroll all to myself an' don't have to share it."

She looked up at me, and danged if she didn't grin. A lady like that, an' she stood there an' grinned at me.

I think I got a little flustered and for sure I felt my cheeks heating up so that they were probably red as a new set of flannel long johns. I ducked my head and tried to straighten out the droop in my hat brim, which I was holding since we were inside.

"Oh, I understand, Charlie. I really do. I know Arthur has difficulty understanding this, but I've become quite properly Americanized, you know."

"Uh, no, ma'am. I guess I don't know."

"I've lived in your country more than seven years now. England is just a memory to me now. A dear and wonderful memory, true, but only a memory nonetheless. Actually," she said it closer to American than the Sir's "ektually," "I've come to be quite comfortable with your wonderfully classless ways. I don't believe I could possibly go back home now, to all that stiffness and class consciousness. Do you understand what I'm telling you?"

"No, ma'am," I said, which was only the truth.

She smiled and took a couple steps toward me, though she didn't look, exactly, like she was gonna deliver a lecture on the subject—which I couldn't figure out and didn't particularly want to anyhow—and was interrupted when the houseman come into the room.

She stopped. "Yes, Julio?"

"Señor Arthur is coming up the drive now, Doña Elizabeth. Shall I serve tea now?"

"Yes, Julio. That will be fine." Her voice was crisper now than it had been, but still pleasant.

"Was there something you wanted me t'do, ma'am?" I asked.

"Yes, but . . . it will wait. Another time, Charlie?"

"Whatever you want, ma'am."

"Would that that were so, Charlie. Would that that were so." Her smile twisted a bit, kind of funny and just a little bit sad at the same time.

"Yes, ma'am," I said again. "You let me know, hear?"

"I'll do that, Charlie. Thank you."

I followed Julio out through the back of the house, not trying to hide from Arthur that I'd been there or any-thing, but it just seemed like the right thing to do. He took me down a hall and out through a kitchen that was big as most houses. His wife was back there taking some fresh pastry things out of an oven—one of *three* ovens, if you can believe that, which I couldn't hardly except that I saw them all in that one kitchen—and Julio slipped me a hand-ful of them, hot and fresh, and gave me a wink. There is something to be said for being on the good side of all manner of cooks, let me tell you, and not just the man who cooks for the hired help.

I carried my goodies back up to the barn and found a shady spot where I could settle and enjoy those pastry things before I went back to my whittling.

CHAPTER 22

Next morning I was outside the cookhouse picking my teeth when the Sir came up from the big house and motioned me to join him. He was walking toward the barn and had a set of saddlebags slung over his arm, so I figured we were headed someplace. Which turned out to be so.

"Better leave the dog here, Charles," he said. "I want you to ride with me, but it might be too much for him to handle."

I reached down and rubbed his head. Like usual lately, he was right there at my heels. "He rides okay," I said.

"No wagon today, Charles. We'll ride rather than drive."

Now that was all right, I supposed, except that I surely wasn't looking forward to straddling one of those big old wide-barrelled cobs for a whole day. Huh-uh. Make you think you was split half in two if you did that.

Fortunately, what Arthur had in mind was to borrow a couple of Miz Elizabeth's saddlers. And let me tell you, I don't believe I've ever set on a horse better than that tall, fancy-blooded animal was.

Anyhow, I tied the dog to a wheel of the wagon and petted him a bit to let him know I wasn't mad at him to be leaving him behind and went back into the barn and saddled my horse. The Sir already had his own saddled, although I'd've been willing to do it for him. That man sure did get around spry for an invalid, though. Never laid off of anything because of it. Today he wasn't even carrying his cane, which I figured likely was because of going horseback and not having any place to pack it.

"Where we going?" I asked once we were in the saddle and lined out to the north.

"I should like to ask your advice about something, Charles."

I shrugged. "Most anything I know, I expect I'm willing to tell." I grinned at him. "*Most* anything, I said."

The Sir smiled. "I shouldn't think this would be anything objectionable."

We rode north seven or eight miles and come to a broad, shallow basin where there was a fine creek running and a good stand of cottonwood lined along both sides of the bank. It was one of those places like you can find sometimes in big, rolling grass country. From any distance you wouldn't know there was anything for miles except more of what you'd been covering. Then you top the last rise, and spread out down below you is a valley watered good enough that a nester could farm it and likely make a living.

On the north side of this valley there were some sharp-walled bluffs, but the south side, the direction we come up from, was nice and gentle and sloping. Off to the west the valley headed up in a tight draw. From what I could see, it just petered out to the east where the ground got flatter. Probably the stream meandered away somewhere to join up with the Beaver or maybe it curled back up to the Belle Fourche, which I understood headed in this part of the country.

There was the usual winterkill cow carcasses rotting in the sunshine underneath the far bluffs and that took away considerable from the prettiness of the place, but all told I would have to say that it was fine. This time of year the grass was already taller than belly-deep to some whitetails I saw browsing near the water, and out on the open ground the grass would normally only get hock high.

There was sweet clover spotted yellow here and there and a whole mess of wildflowers.

"What do you think?" Arthur asked.

"Pretty," I said. I mean, hell, I didn't know what he wanted me to say.

The Sir smiled. "I mean to ask what is your opinion of this valley as a source of hay?"

"Oh." That was different. I nudged my horse forward and trotted down the slope so I could get a better look.

The grass was deep, as I'd already seen, but of course it got thicker and taller the closer you got to the water. From up above it wasn't possible to really tell. Arthur let me lead the way and take my time, staying by my side as I crossed back and forth. After a bit, I pulled the horse to a stop at the creek so we could all water, man and beast alike.

I stepped down and dipped up some clean, cold water to drink. It pleased me to see that the Sir, for all of being a dude, at least knew enough to do his drinking from the upstream side of his horse.

"Good," I told him. "Not too weedy. An' I expect a fella might get two cuttings a year down here if the crick runs the whole summer. Less, o' course, if it dries up frequent."

"What tonnage would you guess?"

I whistled and rolled my eyes. "I'm no farmer, and that's the truth. Never had to pay much mind to hay cutting." I shrugged. "Your guess is at least as good as mine."

The Sir looked amused for some reason. "I thought you were a cowman, Charles."

I laughed. "Firstly, what I am is a cow*hand.* Cow*man,* that's the guy that owns 'em, not the one who plays nursemaid to them, which is what I know how t' do. In the second place, cowman or cowhand either one, nobody in this country hays his beeves."

I explained something about the whys and wherefores

to him and how the cow business works out here. Arthur listened to it, all intent and serious.

"You don't hay cattle then?" he asked when I run down.

"Nope."

"But surely it could be done, couldn't it?"

I had to laugh again. "Lordy, Arthur, I just done told you that it *ain't* done."

"But it could be, I should think."

"If you say so. Fella'd have to hire farmers to get that kind o' work done, though. Most hands, if they cain't do it off a horse, they ain't gonna do it at all."

Arthur pulled at his chin and looked around the valley some more. "Tell me, Charles. If it could be done, and notice that I do say *if,* would this valley provide enough hay to feed a herd of cattle?"

"Damn if I know, Arthur. It ain't the sort of thing I've ever give thought to before. And o' course it all depends on what size herd you're talking about. I mean, a dirt farmer who's got a couple milk cows, he can make out with not so much in the way of hay. But if anybody was thinking of haying a beef herd, well, it'd all depend on how many cows a man was thinking of running."

"Six, seven thousand?"

"No chance," I told him, not even having to think about that. "I don't know much about hay feeding, that's true, but I reckon you could get a fair idea by thinking about the grass that's here an' trying to think of how long it would support a herd standing just like it is. Valley this size, now, you could move a big herd like that into it all at once an' it wouldn't carry them but, oh, three, four weeks before they'd start bawling for groceries. If I had to guess . . . and mind you that's all it is . . . I expect I'd say you couldn't expect any more time than that for the hay you could cut off this piece of ground."

Arthur grunted and fingered his chin some more but

didn't let me in on whatever it was he was thinking now. After a bit he nodded and we mounted again.

Going back we made a loop so as to see some more ground. Found a few more pockets where a man could cut hay, which seemed to be what Arthur was interested in today, but there wasn't any of them very big.

We did cross a wagon road at one point. "This must be the road to Jamesburg," Arthur said.

"Jamesburg?" I'd not heard of the place before, but if it was a town, it was of interest. I mean, we'd been out away from the likker and the ladies just about long enough, far as I was concerned. An evening with the glare of city lights wouldn't go bad along about now.

"The county seat. It is where Elizabeth shops for minor purchases. She goes to Cheyenne, of course, for anything major."

Of course, I thought. Hell, what was a hundred miles or two when there was major shopping to be done.

"You wouldn't happen t' know how far this Jamesburg is, would you?"

Arthur smiled. "Are you trying to tell me something, Charles?"

"Me? Course not." I winked at him, and he laughed.

"All right then. I shan't need you for the next day or two." He dug into a pocket and handed me some money without even bothering to count it. "Enjoy yourself."

"Aw, I better go back to your sister's place with you first. Make sure you don't . . ."

"I can find my way nicely, thank you."

"But . . ."

"All I need do is follow the road south to the track leading back to the Crown B, Charles."

That made sense, so I agreed to it. When I rode off, though, I noticed that the Sir didn't follow the road but cut cross-country toward the ranch. I had to admit that, even though we'd been on a wide swing, he was making a beeline for his sister's place, which not so many dudes are capable of doing in strange country.

I decided not to worry about it and booted the horse into a high lope toward an evening in town.

CHAPTER 23

There wasn't a whole heck of a lot to Jamesburg. About the only excuse I could see for putting a town there was that it was on some water, a thin trickle of the stuff that I took to likely be the upper reaches of the Belle Fourche, seeing as how it flowed away to the northeast.

There were a few houses, a few stores, the usual assortment of small shops and smithy and the like, and of course a fair number of entertainment parlors of one variety or another. Set right in the middle of the whole thing on a beat-down patch of dirt that might someday become a town square if the place survived long enough, there was a structure that was still one-story soddy at the back and two-story stone on the front end. That one had a granite arch over the front door with Clark County Courthouse carved into the stone. They weren't real far along, but they were trying.

What they needed, of course, was a railroad. There wasn't one, but a telegraph wire strung on flimsy poles stretched off toward the north someplace into Montana or maybe over into Dakota. I guess these folks were being just as modern as they could be.

It wasn't dark yet when I got there, but my belly said it was long past the lunchtime that I'd missed and that a bit of supper would not be amiss. I tied the Crown B horse to a rail and went into a place that proclaimed itself the "Best Diner from Deadwood to Buffalo." *Only* one too, I thought after eating there.

One thing turned out nice about that meal, though.

When I dug into my pocket to pay for my dinner, I brought out the coins the Sir had handed me. He hadn't counted them when he gave them over, and I hadn't neither. Just shoved them into my pocket with a thank-you, so it wouldn't seem I was examining them to see had he given me enough.

Enough? He'd gone and dropped two eagles and a double into my palm. Forty gold dollars for cryin' out loud. The Englishman had to be as weak in the head as his cane said he was in the limbs.

Well, I was feeling considerable better after a meal, even after a poor one like that, so I left the horse tied where it was and ankled on down the street to the nearest saloon.

It was just coming dusk then, but already the place was fairly busy, a reminder that town folks, even in small towns, don't have the same can-see to can't-see working hours that a country boy puts in.

I found a soft-looking spot for my elbow on the bar and had a beer, and as that one went down nice I had another.

There was a card game going on in a corner, and you could see from the way the boys was dressed that it was a game being played for fun and no sharpers invited. I sat in on it for a time and only lost a dollar and a half, which is almost like winning the way I play the game. A couple of the fellas dropped out and I joined them as the ones left playing were the ones who'd been getting all the good cards for the past hour or so. By then, of course, I needed another beer.

I was at the bar collecting that when a couple fellas I'd seen before came in.

They saw me about the same time I seen them, and quick as you please, they both got a puffed-up, hackles-raised look to them that for just a second there almost got me to wishing I was small enough to not stand out so in a crowd.

"You sonuvabitch," the one of them said.

He did not sound friendly when he said it.

CHAPTER 24

It was that Dan again and the other fella whose name, if I'd heard it, I sure couldn't recall now, the one with the tender hand.

"My-oh-my, I do hope it's me you're talkin' to," I told them with a grin. I mean, there's lots of things I'm scared of. Snakes, for instance, and ornery cows when I'm caught afoot. But a couple fellas in a barroom, well, that ain't on my list.

"You sonuvabitch," the guy with the sore hand said again.

My grin got bigger. "Foul-mouthed and feisty for such a little fella aren't you. You might wanta take care so I don't get peeved."

By this time, we for sure had the attention of everybody else in the place. Fellas were backing away on all sides so that the middle of the room was mostly empty and the wall space was real popular.

The one with the sore hand made a swipe at his holster, but he come up empty because his gun was back in the wagon laying beside the one I'd taken away from Dan the first night I saw this pair. I would have brought both the things into town to leave them for their owners except of course I hadn't known when we set out that I'd be having the night off.

Anyway, this old boy come up empty when he tried to draw a gun that wasn't there, and then his partner Dan tried it, the difference being that he had a second pistol or had borrowed one or something.

"That man isn't armed," someone said from the side of the room. Whoever that fella was, I was grateful to him, for of course he was right.

Dan's jaw hardened and his eyes looked cold, but there wasn't much he could say to dispute it. And there were an awful lot of witnesses to this disagreement.

"Wally?" Dan asked.

The one whose hand was already sore nodded, and Dan unbuckled his gun belt and came across the room—not too close, mind—to lay it on the bar. While he was doing that, his friend Wally was sidling around so that, either way I wanted to turn, there would be one of them at my back.

Shee-oot. This was a game I'd played before, thank you. I leaned back against the bar and waited for them to do whatever they wanted. I was still grinning and I guess didn't look much worried, and of course that sort of thing can get a fella's goat mighty quick. Which I have to admit is why I was doing it. I was discovering that I really didn't like these boys much.

Dan put his dukes up and shuffled and feinted some, and over on the other side of me, Wally was doing the same thing. They stayed well out of reach while they were doing all this, and I didn't believe it much anyhow. Dan had already showed himself to be a kicker that first night, and with a sore hand I was willing to bet that his buddy would be too. So I stood there and let them show off for the crowd, which is all they were really doing.

I couldn't help but notice that both of them were really looking more at each other than at me. They had something in mind.

I stood where I was and waited for them to get to it.

Dan nodded, just a quick little up-and-down bob of his chin, and over to my right, Wally stepped forward with his fists churning. About half a heartbeat behind, Dan started coming in.

Now what they were expecting me to do, of course, was to turn and try and block Wally's punches while Dan came up behind and planted a boot into me.

Well, Wally wasn't about to throw no punches, and I wasn't about to let myself get caught that easy.

I made as if to face Wally, gave Dan time enough to get where he wanted to be and then side-stepped real quick and took a swipe down and back with one hand.

Sure enough, ol' Dan's boot was coming up just about the time my hand was going down.

I took a handful of pants bottom and jerked, and Dan went down hard.

Now the floor of this saloon was sawdust covered, but there was some hardwood timbering under it and neither the sawdust nor the back of Dan's hat was enough to make much of a cushion. His head thunked down with a sound like a dropped melon, and he let out a groan.

Wally was still coming, throwing a kick of his own now, although at a place where I wasn't standing anymore, so while I still had a good hold of Dan and had him in motion, I just kept on swinging with him.

Dan was startled enough and hurting enough that he'd stiffened up pretty rigid, so I was able to swing him around like a stick. I pitched him underneath his partner and swept Wally's leg out from under him, the other still being high in the air with that kick he'd missed landing, and next thing you know, they were both down on the floor wallowing in the spit and the sawdust with Wally laying on top of Dan and both of them wiggling and cussing and getting in each other's way as they tried to come to their feet again.

The crowd who was watching all of this got a deep-down belly laugh out of that. Those local boys was laughing and pointing and holding their sides. Which I don't think contributed a whole lot to Dan's and Wally's humor.

They got red in the face and sorted themselves out and

come to their feet finally so that they were facing me again. Wally kept glancing past me to the bunch of folks who were watching, but Dan was truly and properly pissed.

Wally stayed where he was, not wanting to be the butt of more laughing I think, but Dan was past caring about very much except that he wanted a piece of me to bite on.

He threw himself forward, fists balled and a mean look to him. He was serious now, and if he'd had his gun on or a knife on his belt, I expect I'd have been in for some trouble. Fortunately for me he was too far gone in his mad to be thinking about grabbing for the gun of his that was still laying on the bar. I was in front of him, and he was gonna plunge straight at me, come hell or high water.

What he got was more hell than high water.

I mean, this was three times these boys had been troublesome, and fun only goes so far.

I swatted his punches down with a forearm and let him have one smack on the button.

I could feel the cartilage in his nose crunch, and you could hear it plain in the quiet that had come over the place when Dan made his charge.

Dan's eyes rolled back in his head, and his head snapped backward while the rest of him continued forward, and he flipped over backward so that he was sprawled onto the floor again.

He was gone like a lamp that's been blown out, and for just a moment there, I worried that maybe I'd hit him too hard without thinking. I felt better when I seen that his chest was still moving.

I looked past him toward Wally, but he got kinda pale and backed a half step away. He didn't want a dose of what Dan had just got.

This time there wasn't any laughing in the crowd. Somebody came over to see to Dan, and after a moment, Wally moved forward to join him.

I backed a couple steps away and angled near to the bar. Without being obvious about it, I reached over and pushed Dan's gun belt so that it dropped down behind the bar where neither Wally nor anybody else would be grabbing it up without thinking. Then I touched my hat brim to the bartender, who was watching but didn't look particularly annoyed by any of this—there hadn't been any damage to his place, after all, just to Dan and to his and Wally's pride—and slipped outside.

I'd had about enough fun in town for one night, I decided.

CHAPTER 25

I woke late that next morning, the sun already up long enough to turn the inside of the little house-on-wheels into an oven, and I expect I wouldn't have wakened even then, except that the dog was licking my face and wriggling in the hind end. He had to go outside.

"Awright, I'm comin'." I weaved upright and found that my head was thumping and I had a foul taste in my mouth. It had been—I don't know—awful late when I got back, and I guess I'd taken on more beer than I'd realized the night before.

Which is not trying to make any excuses for how hard I'd hit that Dan fella. Just a simple truth.

Anyway, I let the dog out and rubbed at my face some. Needed a shave, but I sure didn't feel like standing that close to a razor in my hand just yet. I settled for pulling my clothes on and going out. My, but that sun was bright on the eyes. Maybe I groaned and flinched a little.

There was a sound of chuckling and then a bright an' altogether too cheerful, "Good morning."

It was Coosie. He had pulled a chair out front of the cookhouse and had it leaned back against the wall while he basked in the sunshine. I gave him a weak excuse for a smile and a limp wave. For some reason, likely the way I looked just then, that made him laugh.

"I saved you some breakfast," he said, still sounding so cheerful I gave thought to throwing something at him. Might have, except I wasn't sure I could keep my balance if I tried to move quick.

"Coffee?" It came out sounding more like a croak than a word.

He laughed again. Dang him. And got up. "Set here. I'll bring it to you." Maybe he was a pretty nice man after all.

The dog came back from its morning run looking every bit as chipper and cheerful as Coosie was and walked beside me while I made my way slow and easy over to the chair and lowered into the thing.

Coosie came back out with a mug of steaming Arbuckle's. Just the smell of it was enough to put me on the road to recovery. He saw the dog laying by my feet there and went back inside for a moment. This time, when he came out, he set a plate down with what I guessed was supposed to have been my breakfast. I was grateful to Coosie for feeding the dog and grateful to the dog for keeping that cold, greasy stuff out of my stomach.

"Thanks."

"Sure." He leant down and gave the dog a scratching behind the ears. The dog accepted the attention just fine, but I have to admit that I felt a twitch of satisfaction that once Coosie straightened up, it was my foot the dog laid its head back onto. Coosie went inside again and came out with another chair.

Oh, that coffee was good.

"Got in kinda late last night," he observed.

"You tryin' to rub it in or what?"

He laughed.

"Sorry if I woke you."

"Naw. I was already awake. Thought I heard something in the night an' got up to see what it was. Must've been my imagination, though. I never saw anything. Then after a bit you came riding in. Never made any noise about it, though, so it wasn't you."

That didn't surprise me any. When you've followed cattle up the trail and come in all hours off night herd, you just naturally learn to move quiet when you come into camp. It's either that or get a boot thrown at you or worse. It's a habit that seems to hold, drunk or sober.

I tasted some more of that coffee, finished it and went inside for a refill.

It was already doing me so much good that I began to wonder if maybe it was such a good idea to let the dog have the breakfast Coosie'd saved for me.

I yawned and stretched and carried the second cup outside again. When I got out there, the Kid was there, red in the face and looking like he'd just run a foot race. Looking plenty worried too.

He had to try twice before he could spit out what had him so upset.

After that, I wasn't thinking about coffee or food again for a time.

CHAPTER 26

"The . . . the horses." The Kid was still panting and heaving for breath. "They're dyin'."

I naturally looked toward the corral. Coosie looked toward the barn. We were both wrong.

"Out . . . out in the trap," the Kid panted. "They're keelin' over like flies." He looked like he was halfway to crying, but of course he didn't.

"Go an' tell Miz Elizabeth," Coosie snapped before he headed for the fenced-in horse trap that took in the uppermost part of Quail's valley, up behind the headquarters buildings.

"And the Sir," I said and followed Coosie at a run, us going that way and the Kid stumbling down toward the house.

Jim was already up there. I guess it had been him and the Kid that had discovered the problem and crippled-up Jim had sent the younger legs flying to pass the word.

There was damn sure a problem, all right. There was thirty-five, forty head of the finest-looking saddle stock a cowboy ever did see being held in that trap, but now more'n half of them was already down flat on the ground and those that was on their legs was wobbling around like they were drunk.

While I watched, a sleek chestnut with a mane and tail like flax staggered a couple steps, dropped to its knees and fell over sideways with a grunt of pain.

And horses just don't *show* pain, hardly. For the most part they will stand quiet and die after the awfullest kind of wreck has happened to them. They just don't make noise about it like humans will. For a horse to grunt from pain it has to be a terrible thing.

I slipped through the fence wire and Coosie right alongside of me and we ran to where Jim was standing with a blank, awful, helpless look on him.

"What the hell is happenin' here?"

"I don't know. I just . . . don't know." Jim looked like he was about ready to cry too, and I can't say that I blamed him. Anybody that cares a thing about a horse couldn't hardly see this happening and not.

A dark bay with pain-filled eyes and a fine, noble head came staggering to me like it was asking me to stop the hurting.

And there wasn't nothing I could do for it.

"Jesus," I blurted. "They act like they're all sand-colicked. Walk 'em. We could try walking them."

"There's no damn sand colic up here," Jim said.

I expect he was right about that. Sand colic happens when horses graze poor grass in loose sand, like they have down along the Gulf coast, so that they pull and eat roots and all and everything left clinging to the roots, and after a time the sand they eat packs up in their guts and can't pass and sometimes you lose an animal to it. But so many all at once? And in country where the ground is firm? Still, it was the only thing I could think of. And sometimes if you keep a gut-packed horse on its feet and moving, so that it don't lie down and try to roll the pain away and just make things worse, why, sometimes you can get the blockage loose and the horse will live.

Jim disagreed with me—hell, come to that, I disagreed with myself pretty much—but keeping them moving was something to be doing anyhow. He hadn't a rope with him and neither did Coosie or me, so we whipped off our belts and used them to take a turn around a horse's neck and lead the things, trying to keep them on their feet so maybe they'd have a chance against whatever this was.

Every time we'd see a horse trying to lie down, we'd let go of whatever one we was leading and run to that other one, the three of us trying to keep a dozen horses in motion all at once.

All the rest of the animals in the trap was either dead or dying.

Arthur and the Kid came running up the hill with Miz Elizabeth close behind, her still wearing a housecoat, and Julio just behind all of them.

"What . . ." the Sir started in, but there wasn't gonna be time for explanations, even if we knew what the problem was.

"We don't know an' got no time to figure it out. They're hurting in the guts. That's all we know. Gotta keep them moving. Grab a horse and walk it."

I noticed that Miz Elizabeth was the first to jump. She ripped off the cloth belt to her housecoat and took the nearest horse by the neck.

"Julio," I bellered. "We need a funnel. With as long a spout as you can find. An' oil. Mineral oil or whale oil or kerosene. Anything like that you can lay hands on. Gallons of it. All there is on the place."

It wasn't a remedy, exactly, but it was about all you could do to try and clear something in a horse's gut. Slick the stuff up with oil so maybe it would move an' pass through.

Julio nodded and turned back the way he'd come.

"Go with him, Kid. Help him carry it all."

"I got a bunch of lamp oil in the cookhouse," Coosie said.

"Get it. Bring all you got."

He nodded and took off running. The rest of us kept walking the horses. Those that was left. A young gray, a fine-looking filly about two years old, went down to her knees. Arthur tried to pull her back onto her feet, kicked her and hollered and tried his best, but she was down and wouldn't get up again. Even the dog's barking and snapping didn't interest her. She paid him nor anything else any mind.

"Leave her," I snapped at him. "Get that brown over there."

He nodded, not seeming to pay attention that I was giving him orders, and ran to the brown, which was looking awful weak.

Julio and the Kid came back carrying all they could pack of jugs and pails and buckets of oils, and Julio had a funnel that was probably two foot long stuck inside his shirt.

"Over here."

I grabbed hold of the bright bay filly Miz Elizabeth was leading, a young'un, probably not more than a year old. Miz Elizabeth seemed to set particular store by the filly, as there were tears running down her cheeks and she could hardly breathe for her bawling.

"Let me have her," I said.

Miz Elizabeth tried to help me with her, but I said, "I'll take this one. You go keep that colt moving."

I grabbed hold of the filly's muzzle and pushed her head up. She was hurting too bad to want to fight me. I snatched the funnel from Julio and rammed it down her throat as far as it would go. "Pour the oil in. Quick."

Julio wasn't tall enough to reach the mouth of the funnel, shoved high in the air like it was with the filly's muzzle up. The Kid took a tin of mineral oil, pulled the top off it and dumped the oil in. The filly didn't like it, of course, and the Kid and me got oiled along with her, but most of it went down.

"Miz Elizabeth. Keep this'un walking now."

The Kid and me moved to the brown colt Miz Elizabeth had just been walking and dosed him too. Everybody else was still busy trying to keep moving what horses they could.

But it was a losing proposition.

We was doing everything we could think of, but the horses was still dying, no matter what we done.

They went down, gave up the fight and died with their eyes glazing over. One by one by one.

Miz Elizabeth was crying something pitiful, and I was feeling plenty bad my own self.

In the end we only saved four horses out of the thirty-eight head that had been in the trap.

Thirty-four of the finest damn horses I ever seen died there.

The little bay filly that Miz Elizabeth was so fond of was one of them that died.

When it was over, the sun was nearly down and there was a chill in the air that wasn't anything to the chill I felt in my belly at the sight of all those dead, beautiful animals.

We was all stinking of sweat and nervousness and spilt oil.

"We'll . . ." Miz Elizabeth was having difficulty trying to get the words out. She'd put in as hard a day as any of us, on top of being so overwrought the whole day long. "We'll all go down to the house. Consuela can fix us something to eat." Consuela would've been Julio's wife, I figured.

The whole crowd was looking drug out and empty. Like sleepwalkers or something. Everybody turned and started shuffling down toward the house, except I stayed back.

"I'll join you directly," I said to nobody in particular. "I want t' take a look around first."

Arthur nodded and went on. He had his arm around his sister and was half supporting her. Even with help she was moving stiff-legged and slow and like she was lost in a dream—or a nightmare—someplace.

Jim turned back, though. He looked to be as miserable and wore out as I knew I felt, but he turned back to go with me.

"Kid," he called back.

"I know. I'll do the chores."

I hadn't give thought to anything but the problem at hand all the day long, but of course there was live animals in the corral and down at the barn that still needed tending.

I reached down and rubbed the dog's head. He was beside me, as he'd been right along. In a way, I guess he'd worked about as hard as any of us, trying to keep horses moving the best he knew how. He walked with us as Jim and I wearily started along the fence line.

CHAPTER 27

The rest of them were all sitting at the table when Jim and I came dragging in finally. I can't speak for Jim, but my feet were dragging like my boots'd been nailed to the floor. I was that tired.

The Sir was seated at the head of the huge table in the huge-er dining room. I noticed that he was looking kinda uncomfortable. So were Coosie and the Kid, and I suspected there hadn't been a whole lot of casual table conversation going on.

I don't mean to say that Arthur was a snob or anything like that. I mean, me and him got along just fine when we were wandering about the countryside. But I think he and for that matter Coosie and the Kid too were of the opinion that some things were all right at one time and place but not at others. And that maybe a fancy and proper dining room was not the time or the place for the help and the rich folks to be mixing.

Anyway, about the only one in the place who seemed to be comfortable with the way Miz Elizabeth had arranged things here was Miz Elizabeth. And I have to say that I was glad enough not to've been in on the beginnings of this deal. Tired as I was, I think I'd been happier stomping along the fence line than I'd have been back here with time to fret about which fork to use.

Be that as it may, Jim and me came dragging in just past dark.

"Well?" Arthur asked. He sounded like he was maybe pleased to have something to talk about finally.

I nodded to Jim who was carrying what we'd found, and I pulled out the chair Miz Elizabeth pointed me to. Lordy, but it was fine to be able to set.

Jim went on to the end of the table where Miz Elizabeth was—they was her dead horses, after all—and pulled the handful of dirt and grass and oat grains out of his pocket.

I do not believe I would've done quite the same as him, but what Jim did was to plop the whole mess onto the tablecloth beside Miz Elizabeth's plate.

Her eyes went wide, and for a second there, I thought she was offended by the dirt on her clean table, that maybe she wasn't as American as she'd let herself believe. Then she blinked and begun to look curious.

The Sir and Coosie and the Kid stood up and crowded close. Me, I stayed where I was. I knew what it was we'd found.

"What is it?" Arthur asked, taking it upon himself to do the obvious.

"Smut," Jim proclaimed.

The Sir hiked an eyebrow north, and Miz Elizabeth's cheeks colored a bright red while the rest of her pretty face went pale.

"Not anything dirty," I hurried to try and explain. "I mean . . . there's dirt there, sure. Soil, that is. *Earth* kind o' dirt. But it ain't . . . I mean . . . it isn't *that* kinda smut, ma'am." I hoped she understood what I was trying to get across, because I wasn't sure I could get it said any plainer, without saying things that I oughtn't when there was a lady present.

"It's a . . . it's like a mold," Jim was trying to explain. "Like mildew."

"In the dirt?" Arthur asked. He picked up a pinch of the trash Jim had put on the table.

"On the oat grains," Jim said.

"Pick them out and feel of them," I suggested, "then wipe 'em off and smell of them if you can."

Arthur and the Lady and Coosie all picked out little bitty oat grains from the mess and did as we said. The Kid settled for watching what they were doing.

"D'you see the gray smears on the grains?" Jim said. "That's the smut."

"Smut," Arthur repeated.

"Might have a fancy name, for all I know. Smut's what I've heard it called too, though."

"Feel of it," Jim said.

They rubbed their fingers over the grains, and Jim said, "Feels tacky, don't it? Kinda sticky?"

Each of them except the Kid nodded. Then he nodded too, I guess so he'd be going along with the crowd. He hadn't touched any of the stuff himself yet.

"Know what that is?"

"Smut?" Miz Elizabeth asked.

"Nope." Jim looked proud of himself. "The smut, it feels dry and slip'ry. Almost like a dry oil, powdered graphite or the like. The sticky part, that's lasses."

"Lasses?"

"Molasses," I interpreted for the Sir.

"Charlie's the one figured that part out," Jim admitted.

"I don't get it," Miz Elizabeth said.

"It's the smut killed those horses, ma'am," I said. "It's like a mold or a mildew an' it grows on grain sometimes if the grain is too wet when its put into tight-closed storage. It's the sort of thing a man that grain-feeds has to watch out for and be careful of because it's a killer. As you've already dang sure seen t'day."

"But . . . molasses?"

"That's to get the horses to eat the spoiled grain. The smut has a bad smell to it. Horses, even most cows, won't eat grain that's smut-spoiled. So whoever dumped this spoiled grain over at the northwest corner of your trap, they mixed molasses on the oats so the horses couldn't smell or taste the smut but only the lasses."

"This smut, could it have come . . ."

"No, ma'am," Jim swore real quick. "Me and Charlie already stopped to look in the grain bins on the Crown B. There's no spoilage here."

"It was deliberate," I said. "Had to be or there wouldn't have been the molasses added. And it was brought in from someplace else. Most likely from someplace a lot wetter than this country too. This stuff only happens when grain is stored wet an' stays that way. Besides, all your grain on the Crown B is a mix. Oats and barley and a bit of wheat in it. Whatever was on hand when the stuff was bought, I'd say. This stuff is oats through an' through. Nothing else in it. So it was doctored and brought in deliberate to be fed to your horses."

"To poison them," Arthur said.

I nodded. "That's what it comes to, yes. To poison them."

I thought about adding that likely those four head that survived today hadn't done it because of all our doctoring, but just because they hadn't eat enough of the bad grain to hurt them. Probably they were slow eaters or some of those that was just naturally bullied away from their feed by meaner horses, of which there are some in about any herd. But then I realized it wouldn't do any good to make mention of that. Better to let them think all the work had done some good.

I was thinking about that. The Sir was getting mad. Purely mad.

I'd never seen him like that before and wouldn't have thought he had it in him really.

He stood tall as he could and stiff as a poker and didn't say anything. But there was a set to the fella's jaw and a belly-chilling ice in his eyes that'd make a man back up, invalid or no invalid.

"Poisoned," he said in a low, cold voice.

"Uh-huh," Jim said.

Miz Elizabeth dropped the one grain she'd been finger-ing and picked up her napkin to wipe her hands off. Coosie smelled of his again and put it back down with the rest that we'd been able to pick out of the dirt once we saw the place and figured out what had gone on there. It had taken considerable poking and figuring, too, to find the problem. It sure hadn't been the sort of thing a body would normally expect in the dry, open plains country.

Arthur stood rigid like that for another minute or so. Then his fit or whatever it was seemed to pass. He calmed down and just as normal as you please went back to his place at the head of the table.

"Elizabeth, you may ring for dinner now."

The Lady looked startled for just a second there, then dropped her eyes and nodded. She tinkled a little bell that was near her plate and directly Julio and Consuela come out of the kitchen with bowls and platters of overcooked food that was my fault and Jim's but which no one blamed us for.

There wasn't any conversation to speak of during din-ner.

CHAPTER 28

"Those ugly plugs," the Sir said, just as soon as he'd finished his dessert and laid down his fork. I guess he'd been waiting, likely stewing on the whole thing while he ate, although he hadn't showed any of it and had seemed perfectly normal the whole meal through.

It took me just a second to figure out what he meant by "ugly plugs," though. When I did, I kinda coughed into my fist to hide a snicker that wanted to creep out where it could be seen.

Across the table Jim and Coosie were doing pretty much the same thing, looking everyplace but at Arthur. Coosie's shoulders were shaking a bit, though his face was blank.

Miz Elizabeth didn't bother being polite, the Sir being her own brother.

"Plug uglies, you silly goose," she corrected with a chuckle.

"Really? Um, thenk you." Arthur seemed quite unperturbed by the delay.

The Kid, I think, missed the whole thing. He was still stuffing himself with a second piece of cake.

"Anyway," the Sir said, "I should think we can reasonably look to neighbor Harper's plug uglies for the source of the, um, difficulties."

Difficulties. Thirty-four deliberately dead horses. That was one way of putting it, all right.

Arthur was looking down the length of the table to his sister, but it was clear from him bringing it up while we was all on hand that he was wanting to discuss it with us hired help too. Except of course for with the Kid. The Kid was looking to see if there was anything on the table still that was fit to eat. I halfway expected him to drink the coffee milk next.

I cleared my throat and spoke up.

"Wasn't them idjits Dan and Wally," I said.

"Why would you say so, Charles?"

So I told him how it was I come to know where Dan and Wally had been the night the smut-ruined grain was fed to the horses and why it couldn't have been them. That was the evening they was in town getting a lesson in manners.

"They could have been here before your, um, encounter?" he suggested, but more as a question than like he believed it.

I had to shake my head again. "Too far. That woulda put them out here nosing around the trap in broad daylight. Fella up t' something like that wouldn't wanta be seen. Besides, Coosie told me the next morning that he heard something in the night just before I rode in. That fits. He'd have heard either the guys with the grain or the horses fightin' to get to the lasses-sweetened stuff."

Arthur fingered his chin. "Might they . . ." He shook his head and never bothered to finish the rest of it.

"Besides," Jim put in, "that job wasn't done by any two guys with some stuff in their saddlebags. An' it wasn't done without thinking. It woulda taken two, maybe three pack animals or a light wagon to carry all the grain you'd need to poison so many head and do that quick a job with them. I'd say a fella that wanted to be sure of his meanness, he'd want to feed a gallon and a half, maybe even more of the grain for each head o' stock. That's a lot of oats. Bulky stuff, oats. Hard to tote. This wasn't some deal of some guy taking a notion while he was passin' by. This was somebody that done the deed deliberate."

Arthur squinted toward the fancy lights that hung

down from the ceiling—chandeliers, that's what you call those things, I recall now—and thought over what Jim and me had said.

It was the Kid that asked what we was all wondering. "But if it wasn't Harper and his boys, who the hell was it?"

There didn't seem to be any answer to that one, and personally, I was so wrapped up in thinking about it that I never even gave a thought to Miz Elizabeth having to hear that kind of language.

There just wasn't anything I could think of that made any sense.

CHAPTER 29

I like working with stock, helping to raise cows and nurse-maiding the fool things from one end of the grass country to the other. I like my work or I expect I'd go find something else to do that I did like. But I got to say there are some things, at some times, that just about turn a man's stomach. What we had to do that next day was like that.

Jim and the Kid and me put the Sir's heavy cobs in harness, as they were not the fanciest but the stoutest horses on the place at the moment, and used the double-tree and traces off the house-on-wheels to hitch to the dead bodies and drag them away from the trap so we wouldn't all have to see and smell them while they rotted back into the soil they came from.

It was all necessary, of course, but damn it was an ugly thing to have to do.

Thirty-four head of extra-fine horseflesh turned into food for the coyotes and the magpies.

It wasn't the sort of thing that a man likes to do.

Still, it was necessary and so we got it done.

The Kid let down a gap in the wire at the far end of the trap while Jim and me rigged the double-tree to a log chain, and then we dragged them out and dumped them one by one.

We didn't talk much while we was doing it, and I think even the Kid was affected by the sight of those dead eyes and sleek, wasted coats. At least they hadn't had time enough yet to get to stinking. I suppose that was something to be thankful for.

While we were out there, Jim and me did some looking on the outside of the wire over near where we'd found the remnants of spoiled grain the evening before.

That Jim might've been somewhat bummed up and banged around now, limping and gimping and hobbling like he had to from all the old injuries, but I would guess that he'd made quite a hand in his time. His body was twisted, but there wasn't a thing wrong with the man's thinking.

"See here," he said before I ever spotted the tracks. He pointed to some scrapes on the ground on the wrong side of the fence, where normally there shouldn't have been horses standing as the gate was a good quarter mile off and there was no loose horses let to wander on the Crown B grass.

Now I know that anybody who's ever read any of Mr. J. F. Cooper's stories about Natty Bumppo and friends will just naturally believe that an Indian or a frontiersman can read hoofprints and footprints off the ground like a perfessor can read a book.

Let me tell you. That ain't so.

Oh, I don't mean to set myself up as any kind of frontiersman. Not hardly. But I've spent the most part of my life in the saddle trailing behind critters of one kind or another, and I expect I've seen a hoofprint or two in that time. And the plain fact is, them little scrapes and gouges in the ground aren't half so easy to find or a quarter so easy to read as Mr. Cooper's stories make out.

Maybe it's different back East, where I'm told the ground is soft and moist so much of the time. But in Wyoming Territory and for that matter in most of the places of my acquaintance, the ground is hard, mostly clay or caliche, and unless there's been a rain awful recent, even a full-grown horse won't leave much of a mark. A man on foot won't leave *any* to speak of.

That Jim was sharp, though. He spotted the tracks quick and pointed them out to me.

"They didn't stand long," I said. "No manure piles on that side of the fence." Which is one of the things you look for.

Jim grunted and crawled through the wire to where the horses had been. I followed him.

"Four head," he said after doing some looking.

"Three," I disagreed.

Jim shrugged. "Four maybe three."

That was close enough to satisfy both of us.

"Want to follow them back a ways and see can we find a good print?"

"I'm game," I told him.

The tracks—really just little scrape marks on the hard ground—come from the direction of a rise to the north and went from the north line of the trap somewhere off to the west. Since it would likely be a week-long job to try and follow tracks any distance—and then there wouldn't be any guarantees against losing the whole line of them— we followed them backward.

Jim was better at this than me and was leading the way. He trailed the horses to the top of that little rise and grunted with satisfaction, pointing down toward the ground.

There was manure piles here, showing that the poisoner had stopped for a while where he could wait and watch and make sure he was alone before he come down to do his killing work.

"Three horses," Jim said, coming around to what I'd thought to begin with.

"That pretty much means one man an' two pack animals," I thought out loud.

"Uh-huh. Curious, ain't it?"

"Oh, I don't know. I can't say as I'd want anybody to know I'd done a trick that dirty. If I was gonna do a thing like that, I expect I'd want to do it all alone so's nobody else would know."

Jim knelt down and fingered through the grass. "Whoever it was smokes a pipe," he said. He held up a pinch of lumpy black stuff that left a smear of ash on his hand. "Dottle," he said.

That didn't narrow things much, but it was something to keep in mind.

"Lookee here," I said. Back a few yards from where the man and three horses had spent some time standing and waiting, I found a spot where they had stopped first. One of the horses had taken a leak there, and Jim grinned as he read the message that'd been left.

"A mare," he said, which was plain enough because the place where the urine had soaked into the dry, hard ground was behind the hind legs. A gelding or stallion would piss forward of the hind legs, of course. That was unusual enough, as damn few hands want anything to do with stallions or mares, either one. Either of them is apt to be flighty and distracted when you're trying to get work done, so just about any working hand will only ride a gelding.

But the really good part about it was that the urine had wet the ground on that small spot enough that, when the mare shifted around more, she left a good hoofprint behind. The moisture-dampened clay had taken and held as clear a print as anybody could hope for.

"D'you know the print?" I asked.

Jim shook his head. "No, but I've seen shoes made like that before. I just disremember where."

Both of us squatted by the print and studied on it, trying to hold in mind the shape of the shoe that'd been on the mare's foot.

Nearly everybody makes horseshoes his own little way. I mean, one guy will use caulks and another makes 'em slick. One will turn the tails out and another chop them off square. One might set his nail indents just here and the next man put them just there. The point is, nearly everybody gets in a habit of making them one way and then does it that way, shoe after shoe. Of course there are some as buy shoes ready made, but you don't see so many of those when you get very far from town.

The fella who'd made this shoe made a toe caulk but slick heels, with the nail cuts on either side of the caulk in front and again kinda far back on each side. The heels tapered a bit from the inside so that the back ends of the shoe kinda curved back on themselves just a little.

Jim, I recalled, who did the shoeing for the Crown B, made his shoes slick and with no taper at all on the heels. The sheepman who'd shod the Sir's cobs and left some spare shoes in the wagon when I bought it used heavy caulks front and rear and a squared-off heel.

Now that we'd seen this particular form of shoe, neither Jim nor me was likely to forget it. For sure I expected to be looking for more of the same every chance I got.

Jim grunted and stood up, his joints popping and complaining some when he did it, and turned back toward the trap. The Kid had got done putting the wire back up where we'd had to take it down and was waiting for us.

We none of us had much to say as we went back down to the supper Coosie had waiting for us.

CHAPTER 30

After breakfast that next morning I was feeling low from all the meanness that had gone on around here. I walked down by the pond below the house.

It was early yet, and I scared a pair of mud hens off the water, setting the quiet surface to rippling and shimmering in the slant of dawn light.

I found a bit of wood that'd fallen off one of the trees and threw it for the dog to chase. He sat and watched the thing fly and then looked at me as if wondering if now I was gonna go fetch it from where it fell. I guess throw-the-stick wasn't something he'd been taught to do before. Probably he thought of himself as a working hand rather than a play-partner. He did wag his tail some, though, so maybe he decided my intentions were good.

"Well, if you don't wanta do that, we'll sit a while." I skirted around a flower bed that was showing buds but no blossoms and settled on one of the white-painted, wrought-iron benches.

It was a grand sight there at the pond, fancy and quiet and nice, and I would have to say that maybe there is something to be said for having things just for the way they look instead of only for what they can do.

The dog plopped down by my knees, and I bent over and scratched him some. He wasn't so much of a worker that he ever objected to that.

The grass around the pond was growing nice, watered by seepage I suppose, and it was getting a mite ragged. I'd noticed one of those grass-cutting reel things in the tack room up at the barn and thought after a while that I should drag the thing down here and have a whack at the chore. It would save old Jim from having to do it.

I scratched the dog some more and had about made up my mind to go get the mower when I heard footsteps crunching across the graveled driveway behind me.

Danged if it wasn't the Lady coming down from the house and still wearing a ruffled, frilly robe and an even more frilly nightdress under it.

I don't say that it didn't make me uneasy to see her dressed so, but there sure wasn't any way to avoid noticing. I mean, there wasn't anything *showing,* you understand. It was just the *idea* of it that was distressing. Especially since the dustup with Dan and Wally the other night had put me off my town plans that evening.

I coughed into my fist to make sure she saw that I was there, just in case she'd been able to miss seeing a big old lummox and shaggy dog sitting at one of her benches, and when she didn't jump with surprise, I coughed again louder.

"Good morning, Charlie," she said with a chipper smile that was just about as bright as the morning.

My oh my, but she did look pretty. For any time of the day, not just for so early.

She was still in night things and house shoes, but that dark brown hair was done up pretty as you please with not a ringlet out of place and her lips and cheeks looked like there was maybe just a touch of rouge riding on them, and when she got close and sat right down beside me, well, there wasn't any doubt that she was wearing some of that expensive toilet water.

Which is an interesting thing now that I was thinking on it. I mean, you take some low kind of woman—you know the kind I mean—and they put on toilet water, why, the reek of it walks around ten feet in front of them and is so sharp it just about burns your nose.

This that Lady Copperton was wearing, it kind of floated light on the air, delicate and sweet as jasmine, so that it snuck up on a fellow and got to stirring him without his hardly knowing it was there. Except that it for sure was, and it sure did work. I know that wasn't what a Lady intended and I might have said something about it, except how d'you bring up a subject like that. I clamped my jaw shut and wriggled around, getting just a mite uncomfortable, and tried to pretend that I couldn't see nor smell anything that wasn't ordinary.

The Lady was not cooperating with making me feel any more comfortable neither.

She helped herself to a seat on the bench right beside me and leaned down to scratch behind the dog's ears in the spot that always made his eyes droop half shut.

Sure wished mine would close like his done. Except the dang things popped open wider if anything.

I mean, when she bent down like, that her gown gapped a bit. It was wrapped instead of buttoned. And the wrapping wasn't half tight enough. I coughed into my fist again and tried to make myself look away but couldn't.

The dang dog wiggled some with how good the scratching made him feel, and I wiggled some from how nervous I was all of a sudden getting.

I mean, this was getting *bad* here.

"Are you all right, Charlie? You sound like you're getting a cold."

"I'm fine, ma'am, thank you."

She turned her head to look at me, still bent over and scratching the dog, and believe me it was all I could do to look into the Lady's eyes when she done that. Whee-ew!

"Could I ask a favor of you, Charlie?" she said low and sweet.

I wanted to blurt out that she could ask *any*-damn-thing and be sure of getting it. But of course I never. I coughed again, nervous, and got hold of myself before I said anything that might've been embarrassing.

"Yes, ma'am, o' course you can."

"I happen to know that Arthur wants you to drive him to town today," she said. "And I was wondering, as a favor to me," she quit messing with the dog and laid her fingers onto my wrist; just that little bit of a touch and it felt like I was half burnt from it, "Would you please watch out for him there? I know you will, of course. But would you please take special care today? Someone . . . after the horses being poisoned so . . . I am frankly quite worried about what might happen. Would you please be very careful of him today?"

"Yes, ma'am," I said, and I was proud that it come out like regular words instead of in a croak, which was for sure the way I was feeling like doing. Hell, I hadn't been sure I could speak at all, but far as I could tell, that wasn't noticeable.

"Thank you, Charlie." There was that smile again. Her eyelashes fluttered and she took a deep breath, and somehow I was able to manage not falling off the bench.

She hesitated for just a second and I thought she was gonna say something else, but after a moment—maybe I'd imagined it, it was that short—she petted the dog one more time and then stood. Except somehow, when she did that, it wasn't so much that she was getting up off a wrought-iron bench as that she was flowing upward, she was that graceful about it.

She stood and smiled at me one more time and then flowed back up toward the porch where Julio had come outside, likely looking for her so he could put breakfast on the table.

I took a deep breath to get control of myself then. But I got to admit that, instead of getting up and heading for the barn right away, I sat there where I was on that little bench and watched the Lady the whole way up to the house and inside before I stood up and got about my business.

The grass cutting, I reckoned, would have to wait for another time if the Sir was wanting to go to town today.

CHAPTER 31

Julio came up the hill a little while later with word that I was to hitch up the phaeton. I didn't understand why a man would want to put up with the jiggle and the bounce of a rolling rig when he could ride in comfort, but then the Sir came out onto the porch to meet me when I drove down to the house and I saw why.

He was dressed in the dangedest duds I ever saw outside a wedding party. A light gray suit that prob'ly cost a working man's yearly wage, a pearl-gray top hat, bright shiny shoes with spats colored to match the hat and a stickpin in his cravat that would've made a riverboat gambler's cut-glass tiepin look small. And I didn't doubt a lick that the thing was every bit real.

Most fellows I've known, including every rich man I've ever worked for, could put on a rig like that and folks would go right past the snicker for the guffaw when they walked out onto the street dressed so peacock-like.

The Sir carried it off just fine. He even looked natural doing it.

A gentleman? I reckon.

Without ever thinking about it, I jumped down off the seat of the phaeton and swung the door open. When he climbed inside the rig, I saw that he was even carrying a different cane from his usual one. This one had a hawk's beak head that looked like it was made from solid gold and was a dark, mottled wood for the rest of it.

This polite respect stuff could only go so far, of course. I rolled my eyes and whistled.

Arthur smiled back at me. "One wants to display baubles if one wishes to impress the natives, don'cha know," he said with a grin.

I winked at him and climbed back up onto the driving box. We were off to Jamesburg.

This time, I'd remembered to bring those pistols along so I could return them to Harper's boys.

CHAPTER 32

Far as I knew the Sir hadn't been to Jamesburg before, but one way or another he knew right where he wanted to go. He pointed me to the town square, such as it was, and beside it to a building just east of the courthouse.

It was one of those tall, narrow buildings that from a distance looks like a regular false-front outfit, except that it had an actual second floor upstairs. It was just such a seedy-looking thing that it *ought* to be a false front but wasn't.

"Park here, Charles."

Arthur hopped down from the phaeton and tucked his cane under his arm while I clipped the hitch weights to the bit rings. I kinda wondered what he would be wanting in a haberdashery, which was what the store was, especially since as far as I could tell he must've stripped the tailor shops of half of England to find enough stuff to fit in all the trunks and boxes and cases he'd brought with him, but it turned out it wasn't the haberdashery he was interested in at all.

He ignored the hopeful-looking fella who was peering out through the front door of the store and went to a set of stairs that run along the wall at the side of the building, where I'd thought there was a walk or alley between this store building and the one next to it.

Arthur hadn't said any different, so I trailed along behind him. There was a sign posted at the foot of the stairs saying: SELWYN KIRK, ATTORNEY AT LAW.

We went up the steps and Arthur knocked at the door

there twice, real brisk, and then went inside without waiting for an answer. The Sir had his chin hiked high in the air and acted like he owned the place.

There wasn't any clerk or secretary in Selwyn Kirk's law office. Just this little cubbyhole of a room with the walls unfinished and the insides of the siding showing between the studs and a single, kinda grimy window looking out toward the courthouse.

A man in sleeve garters and not wearing his coat was sitting at a desk that was near the whole furnishings for the place, save for a cabinet in one corner and a couple flimsy-looking chairs in front of the desk.

In comparison with Arthur, the fella at the desk didn't look like much. Hell, I don't guess he'd have looked like much in comparison with most anybody else either. I mean, he was not what you would call impressive.

He was still a young man, not yet out of his twenties I'd have said, but his forehead run halfway back on top of his head. If there'd still been Indian troubles in this country, he wouldn't have had much to worry about. No self-respecting Indian would've wanted a scalp like that one. And like as if to balance off his having too much forehead, he had practically no chin at all. The overall effect was kinda like he had a normal amount of face but that the features on it had drifted south of where they should've been.

There wasn't much air in the office, what with no ventilation to speak of, so maybe that explained why his shirt was sweat-plastered and might have been laundered more recent than was the case.

"Selwyn Kirk," Arthur said kinda crisp and abrupt.

Kirk, for that is who the man did turn out to be, got one look at this obviously rich and high-bred client on his doorstep and all of a sudden looked like he was fixing to ooze straight out of his skin in his eagerness to please.

He jumped to his feet and held a chair for Arthur and

practically wagged his tail puppylike for the gentleman to make himself comfortable.

From where I stood, which was leaning against the jamb and leaving the door stand open so's I could get some air to breathe, it was all kinda funny. I wasn't sure but that Kirk would curtsy and kiss the Sir's ring finger if he thought that was what Arthur wanted.

Arthur's chin hiked a notch higher into the air, which I wouldn't have figured was possible, and he gave Selwyn Kirk a look that would've froze one of those hot springs over at Yellowstone Park. He also ignored the chair that was offered and stood tall right where he was, smack in the middle of the office room, with his back stiff as a poker.

Selwyn Kirk had damn sure heard something about Sir Arthur Cooke-Williams. I could see that plain in the way his face changed when ol' Arthur introduced himself. Announced himself was more like it, really. He said it so haughty it almost sounded mean.

Kirk blanched and seemed to curl inside himself. Whatever was going on here, Lawyer Kirk wasn't liking it.

"The papers," Arthur snapped. No "if you please" or "my good man" or explanation or anything. Just those two words snapped out so abrupt they crackled.

Kirk made a fish mouth, like he was trying to draw breath and talk at the same time, and after a moment got hold of himself and blurted something about, "But I can't . . . I mean, Sir, I am the duly appointed . . . that is . . ."

"The papers," Arthur ordered again. Hard and cold and taking no nonsense. I mean, he was in *charge* here.

"But I . . . I have to see the judge. I have to . . ."

"You are discharged," Arthur said, somehow managing to get his chin even higher and his stare even colder so that now you would think he could barely see Mr. Kirk for tilting his head so far back. "As of this moment."

Well hell, if the Sir ever wanted to fire me, I would sure

believe it if he said it to me like that. Whoo-wee! No doubt in my mind, that was for sure.

Kirk looked like he was fixing to cry. He settled for wringing his hands and then turning toward the little cabinet in the corner. He opened the top drawer and pulled out a thick folder that even from across the room I could see was near about the only thing in that drawer. Without a word, Kirk handed the papers over to Arthur.

No "thank you." No looking it over. Nothing like that. Arthur looked like he was growing taller and stiffer. He clicked his heels together—I swear that he did, which was something I'd heard of before but never seen a man do before—and made a quick about-face that was absolutely soldier like.

He marched out of Selwyn Kirk's shabby little office with a look on him like he'd just had a taste of something that'd gone bad.

Behind him, Kirk was looking like Arthur had just punched him in the gut, although of course Arthur never touched him. Nor needed to.

Whoo-wee. This was kinda interesting.

Kirk made another fish mouth, then blinked. Of course he didn't have anything to say to me.

The lawyer looked like a man who'd just lost his best friend.

Me, I winked at him. Don't know why I done that, but I did. Then I quit holding up the door frame and followed Arthur back down onto the street.

CHAPTER 33

"What you have there, Charles," Arthur said as he climbed back into the phaeton, "is a situation where in the power of greed has overcome that of probity."

He actually used those words. "Wherein." "Probity." Actually did. I'd never known a man before who could string two weird words like that into one and the same sentence and sound like he wasn't showing off, but the Sir managed it just fine.

"If you say so," I told him. I dropped the hitch weights onto the floor and hauled myself onto the driving box out in front of him.

Arthur smiled. "Of course. You could have no idea what that was about, could you?"

"Can't say as I could," I told him and made a resolve to myself to mind my own business.

Maybe I sounded like my nose was out of joint or something—which I hope it wasn't—for he leaned forward and said, "Find us a suitable restaurant, would you, Charles? We shall have dinner before we drive back."

There wasn't a whole lot to choose from in Jamesburg, of course, but I found what would likely be the best place in town to eat if not quite the only one and stopped there. To my mind it was plenty fancy enough, although it would be hard telling what the Sir might think of it. He never said, anyhow.

Arthur went inside while I took the team to water and then settled them outside. By the time I got inside, there was two places laid at a corner table and two glasses of wine set out there, so I figured I was to join Arthur and did. For some reason I guess I was feeling just a little bit tetchy on the subject of plain or fancy this day.

"I haven't meant to keep you in the dark, ektually," Arthur said, once the waiter had took our orders, well, Arthur's orders really, since he went and spoke up without waiting for me to say anything, and had gone out of earshot. "Quite the contrary." He smiled again. "For some reason, Lady Elizabeth deems your opinions, um, of value."

Now I didn't know what all he was meaning by that, but I wasn't going to argue with the man. I kept my mouth shut and my ears open, which often is a good way to have it.

"Mr. Kirk," he explained, taking a sip of the ruby-colored wine while I ignored mine, "was named executor of Edward's estate."

"This Ed bein' Lady Copperton's dead husband," I put in.

"Yes, of course. My now deceased Colonial brother-in-law." He said that with a hint of smile, but whatever the funny part was, it passed me by.

"As I was saying, however," he went on, "Solicitor Kirk was named Edward's executor. I am sure the choice seemed logical at the time. Since then, however, it appears that Mr. Kirk's good offices have been suborned by Mr. Harper or his agents."

I chewed on that a bit—there wasn't anything else on the table to chew on yet—and finally thought I had all that figured out and broken down into real words.

"What you're saying is that that Harper fella got a rein on Lawyer Kirk and Kirk's been running wherever Harper wants t' ride him?"

That seemed to tickle Arthur for some reason. He tossed his head back and laughed. "Precisely, Charles. Precisely."

The waiter brought some rolls. It was about time too. I was getting hungry. I broke one of them open and slathered it with real butter, which beats the lard you generally get whilst trail herding, and set about filling my hollow.

"An' this morning," I said, "you fired Kirk."

Arthur nodded, looking pleased this time.

"So now what?"

"Ah, that is the rub, Charles. Now what indeed?"

"Look, Arthur, I don't pretend t' know what all is goin' on around here. An' maybe it ain't my place to anyhow. But just what's the problem?"

Arthur fiddled with buttering a roll and putting jam on it and seemed to be doing some thinking. After a bit he leaned forward and looked me square in the eyes, ignoring the roll he'd spent so much time fussing with.

"It may be only, um, proper that you become aware, Charles," he said finally. "The Crown B ranch operation was developed with my sister's private resources. By her husband, of course. Everything quite on the up and up, you see."

"You're saying that Miz Elizabeth went and bought this Ed a ranch t' run?"

"No. Absolutely not," Arthur said. "The ranch itself was in existence well before the marriage. The facilities' improvements and upgrading of the stock alone were undertaken with Lady Copperton's resources."

I didn't understand why he was telling me this family stuff, but I couldn't say that I minded all that much. Hell, I was curious. That is what it really come down to. I was curious and he was in a mood to talk about it. Maybe he was really just wanting to think about it out loud. I know I've done that myself sometimes, not really knowed what I really thought about a subject till I found myself telling it to somebody else. Or maybe there was some other reason

that I didn't figure. Whatever, I was willing to listen to
what the man was saying.

"The problem, of course," he went on, "is that the livestock holdings were virtually wiped out this winter past."

I grunted. There were a lot of good men got wiped out
this past winter, as any ride through Wyoming would
surely show, and some of them like Ed Copperton got
wiped out right along with their cows.

"The, um, family hoped afterward that Elizabeth would
return home."

Now I wasn't so sure that I did want to hear any more,
but Arthur was still in a humor to talk.

"Suggestions were made," he said. "And ignored. Elizabeth persists in the belief that her place remains here. She
refuses to come home." He frowned.

Well, I could understand that, I suppose. Way the hell off
and gone in the middle of Wyoming Territory, by herself,
is not the place you would want to put a lady, much less a
Lady.

"It was suggested that I make the trip here to . . .
reason with her," the Sir said. He was frowning again.
"She refuses to listen to reason. She persists in the belief
that she could continue operation of the Crown B, even to
the point of prosperity, if she had capital enough to restock the range."

"Why, a . . ." The waiter came with a double armload
of platters and dishes and another fella behind him to tote
what the first one couldn't. This all for just the two of us.

They took their time about spreading food out for near
an acre about us. I clamped my jaw shut until they was
gone.

"You were saying?" Arthur prompted then while I was
helping myself to some of the duck and wild rice he'd
insisted on calling for.

Now what I'd been gonna say, without really taking the
time to think about it, was that a woman alone couldn't

handle even a small cow spread. And a big ol' sprawling layout like the Crown B? Shee-oot.

Now that I'd thought about it, though, I realized that that wouldn't be a very polite thing to say to the Sir about his very own sister. Figured maybe I should be more dip-lo-matic (I got that one right) about it.

"I was just gonna say," I told him, "that a place hit hard as the Crown B was can recover, sure, but it'd take an awful amount o' money to get it back on its feet."

"How much money?" Arthur asked like he was actually interested.

I had to shrug again. "Hell, Arthur, I ain't given any thought to something like that. I mean, it's not the sort o' thing that would be my place . . ."

"Never mind that, Charles, please. I accept that you have not given it thought. I presume that you could."

"Sure. I expect so. But I couldn't just pop something right off the top of my head."

"You have seen the grazing and hay potential of the land," he said.

I had to agree that I had.

"You know the approximate extent of the holdings."

"More or less," I confessed, which come from talking with Jim and Coosie.

"You are familiar with the, um, requirements of labor involved."

That one was no problem. I grew up in this business.

"None of this, of course, I understand myself," Arthur said. "You have the advantage of me here."

I shrugged again. Can't argue with what's true.

"Would you give the question some thought, Charlie?"

"Sure," I told him. I have to say, though, that I was wondering why all of a sudden it was Charlie again. The Sir just didn't do that so much.

He let the conversation lay there and concentrated on

getting around his dinner then. I did too. I would have to say that I ate good when Arthur was buying.

Afterward I left him to do a little shopping in town while I went over to the saloon to leave those guns for Dan and Wally and then sat in the phaeton and waited for Arthur to show up ready for the drive back to the Crown B.

I still couldn't figure why he'd been so talkative over dinner, but I had said I would put thought to what he'd asked and I did that.

Even went and bought a Denver newspaper not so long out of date so I could read up on the market prices for beef.

He'd asked me to do something, and I was taking it serious, even if I didn't understand it.

CHAPTER 34

"Is there somethin' you haven't been telling us?" There was the sound of a smirk in Coosie's voice. I didn't have to be looking at him to see it. And I could tell, without looking too, that that dang Jim would be rolling his eyes or doing something else to make himself funny at my expense.

"Just doing what I'm told," I said and went right on with slicking back my hair with the comb and bit of mirror I'd borrowed from Coosie.

"Lah-de-damn-da, huh?" I could hear Coosie snicker and Jim whisper something to him.

Well, that was all right. I'd've done the same sort of thing if I'd been a part of this outfit and not just some passer-through. The Kid would've been in on the fun they was having too, except that he'd taken a horse and gone to town for the evening.

What they was funning me about was that just before dark Julio walked up from the house to say that I was expected to dine—that's the way he put it, dine—with the gentry tonight. Invited to show up at nine o'clock if you can believe that. Nine o'clock at night to show up for dinner. Seemed like an awful uncivilized hour for it. But of course I hadn't any choice but to show and to do it when they wanted me to.

Coosie—I got to say this for him—he fixed me up with a little hold-me-over while the rest of them was eating. Then the Kid took off for town and I got myself a bath, and Jim and Coosie sat around making fun of me.

I'd have done the same for them, of course.

I finished up and took a last look at my best clothes, which I had put on for the occasion. I don't say that they were much account, mind, but they were the best I owned. I've never been one for playing the dandy when it come to what I hung on the outside of myself.

I heard Jim whistle. "Purty," he said. "You want I should loan you my toilet water?"

I pretended a scowl. "You want I should try and punch some sense into you? Notice now, I said try and put some in you. Most times I'd figure to punch a guy senseless, but in your case I'd have nothin' to work with." Then I winked at him. "Besides, what for would an old fart like you be doing with toilet water? You're too old for the ladies. I've heard tell about that."

Jim puffed his chest out—wasn't much there to puff but he did all he could—and winked right back at me. Coosie chuckled, obviously happy now that he could watch without getting jabbed at himself.

I was about as done as I could get, so I left them two old reprobates to their snickering, and me and the dog walked down to the big house.

"You set there and wait," I told the dog. "I don't think this invite was meant to include you too." Then I set myself for whatever was up, took a deep breath and knocked on the door.

Dinner was . . . different.

I mean, this business of eating at table with a Sir and a Lady wasn't much in my normal line of things, and I got to say it was kinda odd.

For starters, there was so much silver laid out around each place that a fella could open a shop and make out pretty good from just what they had spread out around one plate. There was spoons of different sizes and forks of different shapes and a couple knives for each person to wave around, did they want, and hell, I didn't know what the half of it was for. A pocket knife and a fork was what I was used to and a hunk of bread or biscuit to sop up whatever wouldn't stick to the fork. But that wasn't the way they done things here.

If you can believe it, they even started out with a bare plate, and before there was a lick of food set on the table, Julio come and cleared away the empty plates. Just took them right off to the kitchen like there was something wrong with them, except as far as I could see, there wasn't so much as a spot of leftover grease on any of them. Why'd he set them out to begin with if there wasn't any need for them is what I want to know.

Then the actual eating got under way with a bowl of soup. Some kind of runny mashed-potato soup I thought it was. I didn't want to get Julio in trouble, so I never mentioned that mine was so cold you'd think it'd been deliberately iced. I ate it anyway, and darned if it wasn't pretty good in spite of being cold. Vishy-suaz or something like that, I believe Arthur called it.

Then the soup bowls and used spoons disappeared and along came other stuff, one thing after another, but mostly just one or two things at a time, and every time I figured we was done, here would come Julio with another round of groceries. Dangedest deal you ever saw. I mostly kept quiet and tried to use whatever tools Arthur and the Lady were using, and I guess I got through it all without embarrassing myself much. Didn't belch or pass wind or pour gravy down my front anyhow, so I guessed I'd held up my end of it all right.

The very end of it all was some berry tarts of some kind and then coffee. By that point I was groaning, as I hadn't expected there would be so dang much and had heaped my plate pretty good on the early courses.

Anyway, it wasn't till then that much talking was done. Julio cleared the last delicate little plates away and poured another round of coffee and slithered out of the room like he was pretending he'd never been there at all.

"Tell me, Charlie," Arthur said finally, "have you given thought to what I asked you the other day?"

"I expect I have," I told him.

"And?"

"Well, I been looking up market prices outa the Denver papers and such, and I got to say that you're looking at a whole lot o' money to put this place back to operating."

Miz Elizabeth had been quiet and kinda distant through the meal, but now she was leaning forward to hear what I thought. Lordy, but she was pretty. That dark hair and big eyes—I still couldn't decide, were they more blue or more green, turquoise maybe—and not a curl out of place, and a gown cut so low that I daren't look her way too close or too often, or I knew I would start to sweat. In fact, I found myself kinda wishing that she wouldn't lean forward quite so much, that she would set back to do her listening.

"Place this size," I said, "it oughta carry twelve, four-teen thousand head. Call it ten, though, t' be on the safe side against another bad winter. Texas cows, not fancy stuff but range cows that can make a living in tough condi-tions, they're going thirty-two dollars a head, delivered price. That's a lotta money, Arthur. And then you got to restock your horses and hire your riding crew. Got to hire in a haying crew to get the horses through the winter. Got to lay in stores and open your line camps. You're lookin' at four hundred thousand dollars, Arthur."

Miz Elizabeth nodded, like that was just what she ex-pected to hear, and I recalled that day that I'd drove the two of them for the picnic and she had sounded pretty sharp about the conditions of the grass and whatnot.

The Sir fingered his chin and looked at his sister. What he said, though, was, "You still presume this ranch can be operated the old fashioned way, Charlie?"

"I don't get what you mean," I admitted.

"This past winter rather clearly demonstrates that one must be prepared to feed cattle through the winter. Your assumptions continue to be that cattle must be expected to feed themselves by grazing."

"I don't know no other way t' do it, Arthur."

He gave Miz Elizabeth a look that I couldn't figure what it meant, although it kinda seemed an I-told-you-so sort of look. Not smug, exactly, but in that direction.

I shrugged. "That's the way it's always been done, Arthur. Maybe there's other ways. You and me looked this ground over, though. You ain't gonna cut but so much hay in range country like this. Not to support any ten thousand head of beeves, you ain't, even if you could find the equipment and the crews to do so much cutting."

Again he gave Miz Elizabeth a look that hinted there was some private thoughts or arguments been going on between them.

He didn't push it any further, though. He pushed his cup and saucer back, like as if to say that that was the end of the meal, and I figured I was dismissed. I thanked them and got up to leave.

"Charlie," Miz Elizabeth said. "Could I speak with you?"

Could she speak with me? Shee-oot, she could mold me like damp clay if that was what she wanted. I nodded.

Miz Elizabeth come over and laid her fingertips on my arm and walked me out of the dining room, but doing it in such a way that it woulda looked like I was escorting her, instead of its being really the other way around. She was *some*, all right.

CHAPTER 35

She took me out the front door and across the porch and kept right on going, down toward the pond and the white benches.

My, but it was a pretty night. The air was soft and cool after the heat of the day, and there was a near-full moon already well over the horizon so that I could see her plain by its light. That only made her look the prettier, and the shadows it made at the front of her gown . . . well, I won't get into that. The upshot of it was that I wasn't a lick more comfortable here than I'd been inside under all the lights of the chandeliers.

I commenced to feeling warm in the cheeks and my breath, I think, was coming in gulps. At least I was having some trouble breathing, feeling like there was a weight setting on my chest or something. The best I could hope for was that I wouldn't make a complete idjit of myself while she was saying whatever it was she wanted to say to me with her brother not around.

She picked a bench that was in the shade of one of the bigger cottonwoods, and that was something of a help. Her eyes were all sparkly and bright in what light there was, but at least I could look in her direction without staring where I had no business staring.

She set herself right square in the middle of the bench —and they weren't such awful big things—so that I had no choice but to either sit close beside her or wallow on the grass. I tried not to do neither for the moment, letting her sit first and then bending down to scratch the dog some. Naturally he had come along with us once I was out to the porch where he'd been curled up waiting.

"Sit down, Charlie." Her voice was soft and as smooth as sorghum syrup.

"Yes, ma'am." I squeezed down beside her, feeling more than a bit uncomfortable about it, as those benches are small, like I already said, and there wasn't room enough for me to scrunch in without my big ol' shoulders rubbing up against hers.

I sure didn't want to make her think I was trying to be forward with a Lady like her, but dang it, that gown of hers was cut off the shoulder—I believe that's the term the ladies use—so there wasn't nothing but skin between my shirt sleeve and Miz Elizabeth. I guess I done some puffing and sweating there, and to try and ease it, I leaned forward and played with the dog again.

"Charlie," she said, her voice with just a hint of a sharp edge in it.

"Yes, ma'am?"

"My name is Elizabeth, not ma'am, and are you going to play with that dog all night?"

"No, ma'am. Of course not."

She raised an eyebrow and sat there like she was waiting for something. After a moment I got it and corrected myself. "I mean, no, Miz Elizabeth."

"That's better."

I quit scratching the dog and sat back to pay attention like she wanted me to, even though that put my shoulder pressing up against hers again.

Now naturally I figured that she'd brought me down here to talk about the prospects of the Crown B and maybe argue with me about how a cow outfit oughta be run or what kind of prices would have to be paid if they decided to go ahead and restock or something like that.

Instead she cocked her head a bit to one side and peered at me for a moment. I think I was starting to sweat again.

After a bit she reached up and felt of my arm. Gave it a little squeeze, like. "You're awfully strong, aren't you, Charlie?"

I think my mouth gaped open a bit, and I didn't know what to say. I mean, what *do* you say when an absolutely gorgeous high-class lady like this Lady says something like that, right outa the dang blue.

She laughed a little and this time squoze higher on my arm.

"Am I making you uncomfortable, Charlie?" There was a teasing note to it, kinda like she hoped she *was* doing what she dang sure was.

"Well, ma'am . . . I mean, Miz Elizabeth . . . that is . . ." I could feel myself heating up and likely turning red and not just in the cheeks neither but just about everyplace a fella can heat up and turn red.

Miz Elizabeth laughed again, sounding right tickled with herself as a matter of fact, and leaned toward me just the least bit.

Oh, my.

I wasn't exactly sure *what* t' do or think or say, and my mouth worked okay, but nothing was coming out of it. Which was all right. The way I was feeling just about then, if I did make any sound, it'd be a croak or a gasp or something foolish.

It was the dog that saved me from playing the fool.

He jumped to his feet with a yip and stood looking down the Quail with his ears perked and tail up.

"Something's coming," I said.

I stood, glad for the excuse of it, and waited. After a few seconds, I could hear the rattle of a wagon coming up the drive at a high trot.

"Are you sure?" Miz Elizabeth sounded disappointed to be having company.

"Yes, ma'am."

This time she didn't bother to correct me.

CHAPTER 36

The wagon spanking it up the driveway so quick was a light buckboard with two men on the seat. I walked out from under the cottonwood to greet them, and the leggy thing between the shafts spooked when I come into view. For just a few seconds there the driver had himself a handful.

"Whoa. Whoa, you sonuvabitch." He sawed on the lines and the horse made a stab at pawing the moon outa the sky, and I stepped forward the rest of the way and took hold of the gelding's bit so there wouldn't be a wreck.

"Sorry," I told the man. "Didn't mean to set 'im off."

"Well you damn well did and . . . oh! Par'n me, ma'am." The driver quit his cussing right quick and snatched his hat off and so did the man sitting on the box beside him.

I looked around and saw that Miz Elizabeth had come out where she could be seen too now. I guess I wouldn't have wanted to be in that man's shoes for anything after cursing like he done and Miz Elizabeth there to hear. Of course they couldn't have seen her in the shadows where that bench was, but that wouldn't have made him feel any better about it.

"Wilburn," she said. "Henry." She nodded, just as polite and natural as if she hadn't heard a word of it, although of course there was no way she could've not heard. "Would you care to step down? I am sure Julio has coffee on the stove." She sure did look and sound and act every inch the Lady she was.

"Well, no, ma'am, I mean . . ." The one she'd called Wilburn sounded uncomfortable. The other man finally spoke up.

"We aren't just passing by, Mrs. Copperton, and I am sorry to tell you that this is not a social call."

"No?"

"No, ma'am. I am sorry to tell you this, but your man Franz was found dead this evening."

That news hit Miz Elizabeth pretty hard. It took me a spell to sort things out, but it turned out that Franz was the Kid, proper name Earl John Franz, and that was who'd been found dead on the road just outside of Jamesburg this evening.

The men carrying the unpleasant tale out to the Crown B were Henry Adair, who was the sheriff of Clark County, Wyoming Territory, and the man driving was Wilburn Ames, his chief deputy.

They hadn't brought the body along, figuring that Mrs. Copperton would want the boy tended by the barber-surgeon in town who doubled as an undertaker when one was needed. They'd come out to let her know.

Miz Elizabeth took them up to the house and I tagged along for lack of anything else to do, and they went through the whole thing for the Lady and then again when Arthur came out of the study to see what the commotion in the hall was about.

Seemed a couple boys riding in from another outfit just past dark found the Kid laying on the side of the road not a quarter mile outside the town limits. He was dead when they found him, Adair said, and looked like he'd come loose from his horse, likely held onto the reins to try and keep the thing from running off, and the critter went wild and stomped him to death.

"I see," Miz Elizabeth said very low and calm. She was standing in that same stiff-backed, chin-high way the Sir did sometimes, and though she tried to make out that it wasn't bothering her that one of her hands was dead, I could see that she was bothered plenty. She just was trying not to let it show. She had grit, this woman.

Arthur took it the same when he heard the repeat of it. Except with him I wasn't sure if it really bothered him or not. Could be that he really didn't care all that much, not having been around the Kid except for that one day with the horses dying and the evening afterward.

Sheriff Adair looked more uncomfortable than anybody, standing in the entry hall wringing his hat brim in both hands and shifting from one foot to the other like he was feeling as out of his place here as I generally did. Wilburn Ames hung back near the door and after a bit slipped out onto the porch. I'd seen what his trouble was. He was chewing, and there wasn't no place in the hall where he could spit, no cuspidor or anything there.

"I hope we did the right thing, Mrs. Copperton," Adair said. "If there is anything . . ."

"You did exactly as I would have wished," Miz Elizabeth assured the man. "I shall . . . come in myself tomorrow to make the necessary arrangements. Please be so good as to inform Mr. Shelbarger."

"Yes, ma'am. I'll tell him quick as we get back." Adair began backing slowly toward the door, still giving his hat brim what-for.

Arthur gave me a little nod and went to escort his sister out of sight into another room, so I done the duty of being polite and going out to see Adair and Ames on their way back to town.

I did that and would've headed up the hill to the cookhouse to give Coosie and Jim the bad news, but Arthur came out onto the porch just as the officers was driving off.

"Charles," he said.

"Yeah?" I sure wasn't in any mood to chat tonight. I hadn't known the Kid all that well either, but hell, it's always upsetting when a fella goes under unexpected like that.

"I realize this is not an ideal circumstance to discuss it, but what did you tell Elizabeth?"

"Huh?"

"Did you accept?"

I hadn't the vaguest notion what he was talking about and told him so.

"Oh." He sounded surprised and actually apologetic almost. First time since I'd met him that that was so. He blinked and made like he was gonna say something but didn't, then waved a hand in the air kind of feeble-like and turned to go back inside.

I had other things to think about than whatever that foolishness was. I walked slow back up the hill to where Jim and Coosie would be passing the evening and maybe even asleep. I don't know why, but I was hoping they were still up playing checkers or something. It's like it is worse to be woke up to bad news somehow, although I suppose that is silly.

Anyhow, I made the walk slow and draggy, and the dog must have taken my mood because he slunk along behind me with his head and tail low and no spring in his step whatsoever.

I didn't sleep well that night, and I'd bet that Jim and Coosie didn't either.

CHAPTER 37

We all drove into town that next morning.

There was too many of us to all go in one rig, so I took the Sir and Miz Elizabeth in the phaeton and Jim hooked up a mud wagon that'd seen better days and trailed behind with Coosie and Julio and Consuela.

Consuela was taking on about the Kid as bad as if he'd been her own, although I hadn't noticed them being so awful close when he was alive. But it's that way sometimes, of course. You just naturally think more of a person when he's gone and can't be told that you think high of him.

Anyhow, we rolled out early, hardly taking time for breakfast, and was in Jamesburg well before lunch.

Cripped-up old Jim took charge of both rigs and the horses, and I went with the rest of the crowd to the lean-to that had been built behind the barbershop. That was where folks in Jamesburg were prepared for burying.

The Kid—I still thought of him that way, even though his real name had been spoke now—was laid out on a table with a sheet over him waiting for George Shelbarger to get instructions about what was to be done. There was no sign today of Sheriff Adair nor Deputy Ames.

"Mrs. Copperton," Shelbarger said in a hushed, oily tone.

"Mr. Shelbarger." She was holding herself proud, every bit the Lady. I thought she looked a mite pale, though. The back of Shelbarger's shop didn't smell any too good to

me, and I was used to a whole lot worse in that line than
she ever would be.

"This is a disagreeable affair, Mrs. Copperton, but the
sheriff left word that there must be the formality of, um,
an official identification before the, um, deceased can be
prepared to your, uh, requirements."

Miz Elizabeth blinked and didn't look too happy over
that note. The sheriff hadn't said anything about it last
night.

"I can do that," I said quick. I sure didn't want her to
have to go through it. I mean, Adair had said that the Kid
got stomped pretty bad. It wasn't the sort of thing a Lady
like Miz Copperton should have to see.

She gave me a grateful look and a nod. So did Arthur.
He'd already had his mouth half open when I spoke up, so
I expect he'd been gonna do the same thing.

"You knew the deceased well?" Shelbarger asked.

"I knew him," I said. "If it's him, that is."

"It is."

"Then why the he . . . then why do we hafta identify
him?"

Shelbarger shrugged. "There will be an inquest. The
sheriff likes to do things properly."

"Let's get it over with, then. Arthur, whyn't you and
Miz Elizabeth go over to that place where we ate the
other day. I'll do what's got to be done and meet you
there."

"And the, um, arrangements?" Shelbarger asked before
they could go.

"Oh. Yes. Something simple, I think. Do whatever
needs to be done."

"And a, uh, resting place in the town cemetery? Would
you wish to purchase a plot?"

"We shall take Earl back home for burial," the Lady
said. "He has family there already." Which I hadn't
known and may have explained why he was the only

young and able-bodied hand kept on the place after last winter. Him and his family must've had long connection with the Copperton outfit.

Shelbarger looked a bit aggrieved but he nodded.

I waited till Arthur and Miz Elizabeth was gone, Julio and Consuela trailing after them, and mentioned, "You won't wanta be doing any *more* than's necessary, I know."

He gave me a good looking over, which meant he had to tilt his head back plenty, as he wasn't such a very big fella, and agreed that he would do no more'n was needed.

"Let's get it done with, then."

Shelbarger took me over to where the Kid was laid out on the hard planks—not that I suppose it mattered had it been a down comforter he was on, of course—and pulled back the sheet so I could see.

The sheriff hadn't lied.

I won't go into what the Kid looked like now, but it wasn't something a man would want to look at twice.

"That's the Kid, all right," I said.

Shelbarger nodded and began to pull the sheet up over him again.

"Hold it," I said. "Let's turn him over."

"But . . ."

"Just do it, mister."

Shelbarger shrugged. Hell, he was used to this stuff and didn't mind messing with the dead. He did what I wanted.

I leaned closer and peered at the Kid.

"Roll him over some more," I said.

Shelbarger didn't question it this time. He just did it, and I took another close look.

"What I think you'd best do," I said, "is to go and fetch the Sir from that restaurant on the other side o' the square and then bring Sheriff Adair back here too."

Shelbarger gave me a look like I'd maybe lost my mind.

"Mister," I told him, "I'm willing to believe that you know plenty about barbering and burying and doctoring.

But you don't know apples about horses. Now you go an' do what I told you to. An' try to not get the lady upset when you bring her brother away, you hear?"

Shelbarger commenced to look worried, but he hustled off to do what I'd said.

CHAPTER 38

"Tell me if I'm not right, sheriff. Whoever found the Kid brought him in and told you about it, and you let Mr. Shelbarger handle the body while you come out to the house to tell Mrs. Copperton. Is that about right?"

"Well . . . yes. I suppose it is," he admitted.

"I thought so, 'cause a man like you, I figure you'd have spotted this just as quick as me if you'd been the one to take a close look at the body."

He stepped over beside the table, Arthur coming with him, and I pulled the sheet back.

I was halfway expecting the Sir to be upset by the ugliness of the sight there, but if he was, he dang sure kept it under control. Fact is, I think maybe Sheriff Adair looked queasier than the Sir did.

"I'm not sure I see what you're getting at, Mr. Roy," the sheriff said.

"You got to look close, I guess, to notice it. But see here." I traced out with a fingertip one of the dents in the Kid's skull. "See how mushed in that is? Rounded, like. Now I'm sure you've seen men stomped before, sheriff." I said that, although at this point I really wasn't so sure about the point.

"A horse's hoof," I said, "whether it's shod or bare, it's got sharp edges. Leaves more of a crease or a line, like, than a rounded dish like this is. And lookee here." I pulled on the Kid's shoulder and rolled the body over to where they could see the other side. I think the sheriff gagged just a little.

"Same thing back here," I said. "The bashing was all over. And a whole bunch of it. Now I want you t' think about something, sheriff. Every time you've seen a man get stomped by a horse, that animal's only hit him one, two licks an' then was gone. Now I know that for a fact because a horse, any horse, it'll purely turn itself inside out t' keep from stepping on a person or a calf or any other dang thing that's soft and uncertain underfoot. Now ain't that so?"

"I suppose it is," Adair said. He turned his head away as if to ponder.

"Of course it is," I said. "Any horse ever foaled, if it does get in a storm and can't avoid stepping on somebody, all it wants is to get off that somebody or something and get the hell gone. And if somebody, say like the Kid here, did manage to get himself in a kicking contest with a horse, which is a whole nuther thing from being stomped upon, the marks left behind by a hoof would still be sharp-edged. They for sure wouldn't be rounded like this."

"What are you trying to say, Charles?"

"I hate t' tell you this, Arthur, but the Kid didn't come off his horse and get stomped to death accidental." I took a deep breath and blurted it out.

"He was beat to death, Arthur.

"Somebody took a club or stick or tree limb and deliberately beat that boy to death."

Arthur frowned. "You are sure of this, Charles?"

Instead of answering, I looked to the sheriff.

"I am afraid he is right," Adair said, sounding like he hated to admit the truth of it but had to. "I am afraid he is right."

"Gather our people together, Charles. We are driving back to the Crown B. Now." He sounded brisk and efficient and not at all shaky or uncertain.

I hopped t' do exactly what the man said.

CHAPTER 39

The sheriff was arguing with the Sir when I got back with Miz Elizabeth. Coosie had been with her at the restaurant, so I'd sent him off to round up Jim and the rigs and Julio and his missus.

What the sheriff was wanting was for all of us to stay in town a while so him and Deputy Ames could conduct an investigation of some sort. Though what anybody from the Crown B was expected to know about a killing just outside Jamesburg, well, I wasn't clear on that point.

Not that it mattered anyway. The sheriff was doing all the arguing, all by himself. You'd think Arthur never so much as heard him. Just stood there stiff and disinterested and let Adair huff and puff all he wanted. Arthur was leaving, b'damn, and the rest of us with him, and that was the end of that subject.

I could see that Adair was getting riled and Miz Elizabeth was getting upset and the Sir was beginning to look somewhat pinched and tight around the lips, like maybe if he quit ignoring Adair, he would do something to be regretted afterward, so I stepped in and took the sheriff by the elbow and pulled him off to the side.

"Look," I said, "I know you got t' do your duty, sheriff. What's more, we all of us want you to. You know? But you ought t' understand too that these folks are upset. The Kid, Earl Franz that is, was with the outfit a long while. Kinda like he was family almost," which was maybe stretching it or maybe not, I honestly didn't know but just wanted to keep the peace, "so whyn't you and Deputy

Ames do whatever you need to here an' then later on, after things've settled a mite at the house, you can ride out and ask all the questions you need."

Adair thought that over for just a bit and then nodded. "We'll be out this evening, perhaps tomorrow," he said.

"I'm sure that'll be just fine, sheriff."

Adair went off someplace, and the rest of our crowd came up in the phaeton and the wagon. Shelbarger came mousing over toward the Lady with a look about him that said he was fixing to hit her up for payment at a time when I figured she needn't be bothered, so I slipped in ahead of him and smiled and stood real tall over top of him. "Later," I whispered. He took the hint and went off to tend to his barbering.

"I think we can go now." I herded the Crown B bunch into the vehicles and set out for the Crown B.

It was a quiet drive back to the place. Awful quiet, everybody wrapped into his own thoughts. Or hers. I kept wondering what Miz Elizabeth was thinking, but she just sat silent beside her brother without much expression, just this blank, distant sort of look on her like she'd been whopped in the head too and was stunned.

When we got back to the Crown B, Arthur told Jim and Coosie to take both rigs up to the barn and motioned for me to come inside. Miz Elizabeth leaned on my arm and I helped her up the steps to the porch and on into the parlor. Julio said something about fixing tea, and him and Consuela disappeared into the back of the house.

"It was that man's doing," Arthur said when we was alone.

Miz Elizabeth looked at her brother but didn't say anything.

I knew who he meant, of course, but I can't say that I was willing to blame anybody without knowing for sure what had happened. I said as much to them.

"You are soft, Charles." It was a strange thing for a skinny little invalid to be saying to somebody of my heft. "You should know," he said, "that Elizabeth has had the idea that she can recoup the fortunes of this ranch. In fact, she discussed with me the idea of hiring you to manage the operation."

Now that was certainly news to me. Likely it was what she'd been wanting to talk about last night and that he'd been thinking of when he asked me if I'd accepted and I hadn't known what he was meaning.

"I opposed her plans," Arthur went on. "I tried to dissuade her. She has little capital with which to work. It was . . . my intention to withhold from her the family's financial support. A matter of throwing good money after bad, ektually." He glanced toward his sister again. They were both of them stony-faced and stiff now.

"My opinion has now changed. This family will not be intimidated by a gang of Colonial ruffians. We will *not.*" His thin little mustache was practically quivering now.

"The family will invest in restocking the Crown B." He emphasized the decision with a curt little nod. Elizabeth nodded too, but if she was pleased, she didn't let it show.

"You should know, Charles, that that Harper person attempted to purchase most of the Crown B grazing lands or to lease them. He even tried to force the issue by striking an illicit arrangement with the executor of Edward's estate. The Kirk person we saw in town. In spite of all that, Charles, I advised Elizabeth to accept the lease offer. I now withdraw that advice. Those people, none of them, shall ever again be welcome to set foot on Crown B property. Have you anything to say, Charles?"

"I . . . don't reckon I know what you want me t' say. I mean . . ."

"Do you accept Elizabeth's offer?"

"Arthur, I ain't heard no offer. Just talk *about* an offer."

"Oh."

"Charlie, would you please come to work as my foreman?"

I looked at Arthur.

"I waive notice," he said. Whatever that meant. All I'd wanted was to make sure it was okay by him, which apparently it was.

I looked at the both of them, and even with the Kid laying cold on a slab back in town, I couldn't help grinning. "I expect it's what I've always wanted," I said. "T' be foreman of a ranch that's got no cows and no horses and no hands except for a cook and a cripple. Sure, why wouldn't I want t' take that on."

Arthur busted out laughing. Sometimes I sure couldn't figure that man. The Lady got up and come over to stand in front of me, so of course I stood too. She reached out like to shake my hand, but instead of shaking it, she kinda held it for a bit. Like she was clinging to it, almost.

I begun to get that feeling again. The one that I got most any time she was in the neighborhood. The one that was sure gonna cause me some down-deep embarrassment if I couldn't learn to get over it.

"Thank you, Charlie."

Darned if she didn't rise up onto her tiptoes and give me a kiss. She was feeling too wobbly and sad, I guess, to be paying proper attention, and if I hadn't thought in time to turn my head so that it landed on my cheek, she'd have planted one right on my mouth. Which I sure would've enjoyed, but which would've been an embarrassment to her and to her brother both. So I was kinda glad and kinda not that I'd realized her mistake in time.

"We shall have to discuss the finances, Charles," Arthur said. "I have some ideas about how to maximize the family's investment returns."

"Yes, sir," I said, although I'd already told them exactly what would have to be spent to get done what had to be done.

I was about to say something about that when the dog set up a barking fit out on the porch to announce that somebody was coming up the road.

"That must be the sheriff and Deputy Ames," I said. "He said something about coming out this evening or tomorrow. I guess he just wouldn't wait no longer."

Arthur nodded and I went out to greet the sheriff and shut the dog up.

CHAPTER 40

Except it wasn't the sheriff and his deputy coming to call, it was Justin Harper and his usual bunch. I could not say that I was happy to see them, particularly after what Arthur'd just said about them not supposed to come onto Crown B ground again. I guess the headquarters here was about as much on Crown B ground as a body could get.

I hushed the dog and walked down to greet them on the driveway before they might come up to the actual house and peeve Arthur.

"You fellas should know by now that you ain't welcome here," I told them. I was trying to be polite about it and was careful not to let anything nasty into my tone of voice. I was just trying to be helpful and avoid trouble.

Harper gave me a cold, haughty look and swung his leg to get off his horse.

"I truly wish you wouldn't do that," I said and moved a step closer.

That brought Dan and Wally off their saddles, ready to defend their boss. Well now, I couldn't hardly blame them. They was only trying to do what they thought they should, and it wasn't like they were reaching for guns or anything. I mean, I'd whipped both of them together once before already, but they were willing to have at me again for their boss's sake. And I can understand that without getting mad about it.

Harper settled back into his saddle to watch the show.

It was the other younger fellow, the one who dressed

nice and never said anything, who was really looking nasty now.

"You sure you want to do this, boys?" I asked. I lifted my arms and flexed a bit and got set for them to come if that was what they wanted.

Dan and Wally were sensible enough to look to their boss before they went and did anything rash.

"You know, Mr. Harper, I would have to say that you aren't real popular here right now, what with that business with Selwyn Kirk and then poisoning the horses and now with Earl Franz being killed. No sir, I would have to say that it would be better all the way around if you was to stay clear of the Crown B from now on."

Instead of getting mad, Justin Harper looked confused. Which I got to admit confused me too. I'd expected him to bluster or fuss or something. Instead he just blinked.

Then he looked down at Dan and Wally with a question in his eyes.

"No, sir," Dan spoke up. "We don't know nothing about that."

"Now see here, young man," Harper said. "I don't know what game you are playing. And I freely admit that I conducted, um, negotiations with lawyer Kirk. That was all entirely legal and aboveboard. But as for any poisonings or young Franz dying . . . was he poisoned too?"

Damned if I didn't halfway believe him just from the way he said it.

Now I have always believed that talking is easier than fighting. Sometimes not so much fun, mind, but certainly easier. And when folks started dying, well, it wasn't any shape of fun at that point. So I said, "The Kid didn't eat no smut-spoiled grain, Mr. Harper. He was beat to death on the road to Jamesburg just last night."

Harper's jaw gaped and again he looked at Dan and Wally.

"No, *sir,*" Dan swore. "We don't know nothing about that. Truly."

"Wally?"

"No, sir. We carted that spoilt grain off and dumped it. Just like you told us."

Harper stared down toward both hands, but they weren't giving in an inch.

I got to say that I found it interesting to learn, though, that there'd been smut-ruined grain on the Harper place. Leftover stuff, I suspected. It happens sometimes, and when it does, the only thing you can do with it is dump the stuff and bury it so nothing will get into it.

"We never, Justin."

"They didn't," I agreed out loud. "The night the poisonings was done was the same night these boys and me got into a fuss in town. They weren't in any shape to be night-riding, even if they'd had time. Which they didn't."

"And you say Franz was beaten to death?"

"That's right. Beat to death on his way to town just last night."

"Do you know what time it happened?" Harper asked.

I shrugged. "Not for sure, of course. Likely around dark. That's the sheriff's best guess that I've heard. That was when they thought it was an accident. I don't suppose that will change now that they know it was a killing."

"Dan and Wally were at the house for supper last night about dark. My place is a good four hours from town."

"Then they don't have anything to worry about when the sheriff comes asking questions," I said.

"The sheriff is into this?" It was the young, quiet fella who spoke. I thought he was looking pale.

"Hell yes, the sheriff's into it. It was a killing, wasn't it?"

"I . . . wouldn't know."

Harper gave the young guy a funny sort of look.

Then Harper went pale too. "Jesse . . ."

"Don't look at me like that, Papa."

"Jesse, you didn't. You couldn't have." Harper said it, but he sure didn't sound like he believed it his own self.

It seemed pretty clear what had happened. Jesse Harper had thought he was helping out by being mean when all he was really doin' was making things worse.

"You shouldn't have done those things," I said. Which was probably stupid of me, speaking out like that, but I said it before I thought.

Justin Harper blanched.

"He knows, Papa. This big sonuvabitch will tell the sheriff. Don't let that happen, Papa. Don't let that happen to me."

Jesse Harper was looking nervous and excited—and damn well worried, as he sure should've been—and Justin Harper was looking hard and cold again.

For a while there I'd begun to think that he wasn't so unreasonable after all, but he turned hard again.

The dog whined and pressed up against the side of my leg.

"Dan. Wally," Harper said. "I won't have my boy carried off to jail for simple foolishness."

Hell, I wasn't so sure but what I wanted to whine and press up against somebody too. I mean, there was four of them and they had guns. I'm a better than fair hand with my fists but not *that* good.

Dan and Wally looked uncomfortable about what was happening here. But they looked, too, like they would do whatever they were told.

"You can't shoot me down here in the yard," I said. Stupidly. "It'd draw attention and everybody'd see, and then you'll *all* be wanted by the law. Leave it be, man, before it just gets worse."

Harper scowled, and it occurred to me finally—about ten seconds too dang late—that what I'd told him was that if they started shooting at all, they were gonna have to shoot everybody on the place and not just me.

And I wasn't so sure that Justin Harper wasn't willing to do exactly that in order to save his boy from a hanging.

I shifted just a little bit closer to Wally. Close enough to reach him and start doing some damage if Harper gave the nod, damn him.

They might take me. They might even do it cheap. They sure weren't gonna do it for free.

CHAPTER 41

Justin Harper gave the nod.

Damn him.

Soft and low he said, "Take him, boys. Take him quiet if you can. Take him and we'll use a knife."

That son of a bitch.

If I so much as hollered, it would mean the death of all of them at the place, the two women and an invalid and a cripple and a pair of cooks. There wasn't any of them expected to be fighters. And for that matter neither was I.

But it was something that they were wanting to take me quiet.

Without their damn guns this wasn't going to be so easy as Mr. Justin Harper wanted.

Dan and Wally spread apart and moved around to cut me off from running to the house—which I had no intention of doing anyway, as that would only involve the others as much as if shots were fired—like a pair of good cutting horses setting a maverick off from the rest of the gather to be castrated and branded. What they had in mind for me, of course, was somewhat worse even than castration.

Jesse Harper and his papa stepped down off their horses and joined the other two.

They had me boxed.

Dan and Wally had belt knives that they pulled. Jesse dragged out a folding Barlow and took his time about opening the blade.

Me, I had a pocket knife too, but I wouldn't know anything about using it for a weapon. It was for whittling or repairing leather and like that. I'd never in my life gave thought to fighting anybody with a dang knife. I left it where it was, figuring it would only confuse me to start trying to learn new things just now when I had other stuff to be thinking about.

Dan and Wally were the ones I was the most worried about. Unlike me, they acted like they knew how to use a knife, holding the things low and with the cutting edges up.

I shuddered and was wishing I was someplace else.

I didn't want my back to that damned crazy Jesse, but he seemed a lesser evil, so I tried to concentrate on Dan and Wally and keep half an eye on Jesse. The old man, I didn't figure, would be much a part of it.

Wally ducked down into a crouch and moved in a little closer.

I feinted a swipe in his direction, spun and kicked out at Jesse's hand trying to knock the Barlow away from him.

I missed, jumped back and felt a tug at my shirt as Dan's knife swished through the air where my ribs had just been.

Where the hell had he come from?

I chopped down with the edge of my hand and connected with Dan's forearm in mid-slash. It was a good solid smack, and I knew that arm would be numb for a while and maybe even broke. He didn't drop the knife, but I knew he was hurting.

There wasn't time to follow up on it. Wally was behind me.

I spun around to face him, but I was too late.

Wally'd been moving in with his knife low and driving, but all of a sudden there was a low, snarling growl and Wally had himself a throat full of dog.

And the dog was just as serious as I felt.

Now I guess I knew how it is that one sad-looking sheep-dog can fight off wolves and coyotes by the pack.

The dog was driving for the kill, straight for the throat, and there was blood flying in all directions.

Wally screamed and dropped his knife and was trying to pull the dog off his chest, and Dan was trying to help him left-handed.

I turned and faced Jesse Harper, who went pale and took a step backward, not so damned ornery and brave now that it was just me and him and his Barlow in the fuss.

"Come on, damn you." I started for him.

"The hell with it," the old man said and pulled his revolver.

I was eight, ten feet away from Justin, but close enough to Jesse to get at least one good lick in on Harper's night-riding boy.

I tried to ignore the fact that Justin was bringing his pistol up and cocking the thing, and concentrated instead on busting Jesse's face with one solid punch that had every ounce of me behind it.

Then I heard the roar of Justin's shot and felt a punch in the ribs harder than *any* mule can kick.

Jesse's jaw was broke and there was blood streaming out of the pulp that'd been his nose.

But that wasn't a whole lot of satisfaction to me.

I was down on my knees without hardly knowing how I'd got there. I mean, I remembered standing up punching Jesse and hearing Justin's gun go off and then I remembered being down on my knees with a bone-deep ache in my right side, but I couldn't seem to recall a dang thing in between those two events.

I looked at that damned Justin and he was raising his revolver again, and this time he was taking careful aim at the middle of my forehead.

"You old bastard," I said and then regretted that I was gonna die with a cuss word on my tongue.

CHAPTER 42

It was the most fearsome, terrible thing I'd ever seen. I hope I never have to see the like again.

But I'm glad I did, and I'm grateful.

One second Justin Harper was standing there with a pistol in his hand fixing to do me under, and the next it was like there was this awful force that'd been set on the loose.

It was the Sir, little cane-leaning Arthur, and if I hadn't seen it for myself, I wouldn't have believed it.

He wasn't carrying a cane this time but a sword, a skinny, whippy, light little blade, but it wasn't the weapon that was so scary. It was Arthur himself.

I'd heard people talk about cold fury, and I guess I'd thought I knew what they meant. I hadn't. Now I did.

Arthur looked ten feet tall and mean as the Shades of Hell.

He came flying in out of noplace.

The sword flashed in the air, and there wasn't anything in Justin Harper's hand any more. There wasn't even much of a hand left there any more.

Harper was too shocked to know, I guess, that he wasn't whole no more. He stood and gaped, and Arthur's sword flashed again and Harper went down spewing blood.

Jesse dragged iron, too late to do his papa any good, and Arthur went for him next.

The sword darted and flicked, and I won't try and say what it done with Jesse. I hope I never have to remember that again.

The Sir whirled and ducked, and I heard a gun roar.
Dan was on his feet and had his revolver leveled.

Dan was fast and he was tough, but there couldn't anything or anybody stand in the face of the Sir that day. Lordy, I'd have been puking and cowering myself if it was me he was coming for.

Dan fired again, but his hand was shaky and he missed, and the Sir crossed the distance between them like a fierce, deadly thunderbolt, and the sword glittered bright in the late afternoon sunlight.

I felt something at my shoulder and like to jumped out of my skin, but it was the dog there beside me, whining and licking at the side of my neck and wriggling up close against me.

I draped an arm over his neck to keep me from falling flat on my back.

The Sir was standing amongst the dead bodies with this funny, distant look on him, like he'd been off in a dream, or a nightmare, someplace and was having trouble finding his way back.

I looked around. The two Harpers and Dan were dead as winterkill calves. The Sir was looking lost, all of a sudden seeming small and skinny and unhealthy again. He shuddered and looked at me.

I wanted to wink at him. To assure him I was still there. But I saw some slow movement off to the side and turned to see what it was.

Wally was still alive. Barely alive but hanging on. The dog had tore him up something awful so that there wasn't much of him above the waist that was anything but red, but he was still there and he was still game.

He had his revolver in his hand, and he was pointing it at the Sir.

I heard a gun bellow, and Wally jerked. His pistol fell out of his fingers, and he flopped forward for good.

Jim was standing about halfway up the hill toward the

barn with a smoking old Spencer carbine in his hands. Behind him Coosie was carrying a scattergun that he looked ready to use if only there was somebody more who needed shooting.

"I'll be damned," I whispered to nobody in particular.

Then everything started to go dim and fuzzy, and there was a ringing in my ears.

For the second time in just a few minutes, I was regretting that I might die with a curse for my last word.

CHAPTER 43

It was a while before I knew much of what was going on around me. Four days they told me afterward, but I got to take their word for all of that.

Deputy Wilburn Ames was sitting in a rocking chair in the room when I woke up. He was wearing spectacles and had a newspaper laid open in his lap.

I opened my eyes and looked around some and couldn't figure out where I was or what was happening, so I asked Ames. He jumped like I'd just shot him instead of speaking to him.

"When did you decide to live?" he asked.

"In doubt, was it?"

"It surely was."

I was going to repeat my question about where they'd taken me until Consuela came in with a bowl of hot, steaming soup that smelled so fine my mouth started to water and my stomach began to cramp from being so hungry.

She looked at me and jumped too, so I realized it was Ames she had brought the soup for and not me. She set the tray down on the table beside Ames's chair and went yelping and running out into the hall.

So it was the big house they'd carried me to. This bedroom with a four-poster and curtains at the window and Julio's wife serving food sure wasn't anywhere near a bunkhouse cot.

"There are some questions we have to ask you, Mr. Roy, about . . ."

He never had time to finish the rest of it because Miz Elizabeth came rushing into the bedroom with the Sir strolling along some steps behind.

"Leave us alone, please, deputy," she said.

"But, ma'am, I . . ."

"I know. I understand. You will have ample opportunity to ask all the questions you wish. Later. Would you please leave us now?"

Ames shrugged and vacated the place. I heard his boots going down a set of stairs, so they must have brought me all the way up to the second floor of the house, up to the private, family quarters.

Miz Elizabeth sat on the edge of the bed, not causing too much hurt when the mattress was jostled, and danged if she didn't begin stroking my chest and arms. Which I noticed for the first time hadn't anything in the way of clothing on them.

"You were magnificent, Charlie. Thank you." Then she leaned down and gave me a kiss. Right on the mouth. Right there in front of her own brother.

Arthur winked at me over her shoulder and shrugged. "Elizabeth has always had an unfortunate attraction to muscular Colonials, doncha know."

I think I blushed some. Felt like I must have anyhow. And I changed the subject. "If you want magnificent, look at your brother. He's the one charged guns with nothing but a sliver o' metal."

"Arthur? Pooh! He's always doing silly things like that."

"Huh?"

"You mean he never told you? Major Cooke-Williams? He's quite famous in India. Or so he tells me. But you, Charlie. You were willing to face all those awful men with nothing but your hands. Why didn't you call out for help?"

So I explained it to them, and danged if the Lady didn't kiss me again.

There was some scratching and whining at the door, and Arthur opened it to let the dog in.

"He's been at your side day and night, Charlie," the Lady explained. "We make him go outside several times a day, though." She sighed. "I suppose I shall have to learn to put up with dogs, shan't I?"

I couldn't exactly figure out what she meant by that, but I agreed anyway.

"What is his name?"

"Doesn't have one that I know about." I grinned. "Might have to give him one." I reached over and scratched him behind the ears.

"Arthur. How come you carry a cane? I mean, I've thought all this time you're an invalid. But I got to say you didn't much act like one when . . . you know."

The Sir laughed. "A gentleman *does* carry a cane, Charles. A, um, sword-cane, ektually."

"Shee-oot."

"Arthur," the Lady said in a no-nonsense tone. "Would you leave us alone now, please?"

"Elizabeth . . ."

"Now, Arthur."

The Sir might be willing to pick up a sword-cane and go after four gunmen with it, but he wasn't going to stand against his sister when she used that tone of voice with him. He turned and got, meek as you please.

"Now, Charlie," Elizabeth said in a soft voice that was just about as different from that other one as you could get.

"Yes, uh, ma'am?"

Then she bent down to me.

But that's another story.

Old Marsden

FRANK RODERUS

When he was born his parents named him Alvin, but that was a good long time ago. These days pretty much everybody just calls him Cap. Maybe he isn't quite as spry as he was back in his trapping days, but he can still sit a horse and his aim is almost as fine as ever. Most of the time, though, he is perfectly content to regale his granddaughter with tales of his exploits. But when someone kidnaps that lovely little girl, Cap isn't about to leave her rescue up to somebody else. He won't rest until she is home safe and sound—and until whoever took her learns just how much grit Cap still has in him.

___4506-0 $4.50 US/$5.50 CAN

Hayseed

FRANK RODERUS

Arnie Rasmussen is a big guy, with the general build of a young ox, and he might not know much, but he knows one thing: He loves Katherine Mulraney. Sure, she's too good for him; she is beautiful and fine, and he is, well, just Arnie. Just as he is steeling his nerve to talk to her, she disappears. Folks say she up and ran off with a fancy travelling man, but Arnie can't believe that. So he sets off after her. But the Wyoming Territory is a mighty tough place, and Arnie has never been off of his father's ranch. He has a lot to learn, and he'll learn all right . . . the hard way.

___4432-1 $4.50 US/$5.50 CAN